Babel

Babel

Alan Burns

CALDER

CALDER PUBLICATIONS
an imprint of

ALMA BOOKS LTD
3 Castle Yard
Richmond
Surrey TW10 6TF
United Kingdom
www.calderpublications.com

Babel first published in 1969
This edition first published by Calder Publications in 2019

Cover design by Will Dady

Text © Alan Burns, 1969, 2019

Printed and bound by CPI Group (UK) Ltd, Croydon, CR0 4YY

ISBN: 978-0-7145-4917-0

Contents

FOR MY FATHER

Babel

THE LONG-DISTANCE WAITRESS SNIFFS THE COUNTER; she keeps glancing at the sandwiches two miles away. The drunks that pass in the night should not be there; the eighty-year-old waitress fusses over vegetables, busy with fresh paper – painfully working alone at midnight, travelling her years on the street because anyone has to have money at the end of the week and a bed to lie on. The brilliant chef is made of pastry; he is said to make people cheerful at the end of the long restaurant, wading across raw people of the pie and sausage-roll variety, screaming for a great sauce. His curry is bland – it tastes of the mudflats behind the railway station. The beer is pepperless – there's not enough splash in it. Our Father with the flask is a gambler between prostitutes; his home is the Savoy in the evening. The coffee attracted him; the human cannot stand exposure. The bacon and egg pours out, cooling him; he last washed his haddock three years ago; things are better every day. The mistaken impressions of the few people who are still such nice people are those of well-dressed queers on the watch. Father starts the heater, and of course the blue steam starts a person thinking. Some who say they love the night cannot get anywhere in the day. Women look old at five in the morning; the skin business drags on; the young man livens up; actors think it exciting in Earl's Court; the Italian waiter could be brilliant frequently. It's energy takes the money in the gambling business. Here you find friends – good friends arrive for fifteen shillings – a small crowd stays the night. The American woman grows stronger and stronger; a young couple spoke to a chap in a woolly jumper; when people said they were hungry, the silk spaghetti was slung at them; the place made money somehow; each hand was a hand on a quid. During the night the mood shuffled and the changes entered quietly. "I won't drink watered wine." A body is sixty per cent water; sixty in the room are nude – none knowing what would emerge, sitting back or sleeping, though Frank proposed to stay warm this winter. Because of the shape and weight of their bodies, the liveliest women undressed for easy money; the daughter kept naked and drunk for half an hour.

THE FATHER RAPES HIS DAUGHTER, which is something she shouldn't see. The fellow is knuckling down and getting in further. It is hard behaviour from a man with religious grounding. And he expects his son to turn out really bad. The long-haired boy should marry his own; loose skin-colour conventions corrupt the people. The boy with freckles has breakfast, then a long talk; he is worried about Vietnam and insists on having an open discussion on the decent life. The hard father will pass him in his car. The thing about his manner is that the pivot of him is claustrophobic. The constant contact with children has not brought a sympathetic manner during twelve years of family. His minicar is more important. The muscular man in the football club is ready for jokes about sex. Like the painted angels, he renounces the world – except for sex and money. With his ironic neighbours he gives money to the priest and tells his son to learn good manners and agree with Eamonn Andrews.

THE FLORID ADOLESCENT FINALLY BURST OUT; the lid flew off the saintly parent; the hysterical war of nerves – more powerfully restless – concentrated on total inessentials. Studying the dress of love, the biblical teenager sheared his locks; sex

was the worst thing really; poking his thumb in Miss Hueth
(but it was an idealistic thumb).

THE PALE BRITISH CITIZEN AND HIS CHARMING FAMILY...
family of killers.

WIFE WOULD BE HIS TO HATE. The disappointed love was
tears on her cheeks. Her house was unlucky; her child had no
money; there was nothing careful in her marriage. She stopped
at the end of a sigh. She told her husband to accept it for the
moment. He patted the scared girl.

AFTER A TIME HE KNIFED HER IN THE KITCHEN, between
the counter and the machine, as the fork water turned dreadful; the noise from the machine as from eight women; trays
of dregs of purplish colour full of the whirring fan continu-
ally in fever. "It is the blackcurrant jam which makes a noise
five feet wide; it is that which does this, with the little glass
of laughter." The tall woman with the washed-out metal fea-
tures loved like a knife; the shaped and sloping waitress was
peculiarly vicious; her legs got trodden on three times a day.
She said she would not sing, but she refilled her lungs "just in
case"; her plate of hot water beside her, her sterilized eyes filled
with singing, but very softly, with long apprehension. Fatness
is like her husband – all his fat had died – her bosom huge;
her arms, four of them, were good, elegantly tapered, and she
scrubbed floors for friends, ponderously for a penny. She fell in
love with ham and flowers; he would slip notes into her salad;
she turned her head in regret. Her deep-sea face was too shy
to speak in a public park, before the vibrations of summer in
fruit dishes replied. The tea is sugared in the lavatory where
sexual women slip off for a cigarette on Thursdays; the plate
of cakes left on the stairs. Sex behind their hands, deposited
in dirty cups, the English elemental, talking tea; all they talk

is tea; her voice is dissolving sugar, into which she laughs so soft it is difficult to hear or understand.

THE SPRAY OF GRAVEL was delicate to anticipate. The car would not return.

FROM A CRIMINAL LUNATIC SOMEWHERE IN EDINBURGH there are signs that his survey of sexual development in the female knows what it means and determines the sex acts of two thousand people: some of these are symbolic; some make abnormal arrangements; something is wrong with the symbols used by some of them.

YOU CAN MAKE MORE MONEY FROM A GIRL WHO'S IRRE-PLACEABLE. Twiddle the cumbersome girl and make her spin on a rod. It is easy to make her happy with bits of varnished wood. Most girls leave home shiny and clean, then the fear is melted in; the hellish environment makes them mad. They are quite good-looking, endlessly smearing handfuls of clay over their legs till they're black from top to bottom. The bright manager examines seventy-two girls for three weeks, and there's no complaint. The red-hot girls have gone to America; two thousand are in demand; northern novelties come in teams of four; they can be bought in antique shapes – globular brown, and crumbling tan. The froth flies off into the foreseeable future, silence waits for an answer. Future advance depends on America.

HOUSEWIVES COMPLAIN THROUGHOUT THE UNITED STATES; they can't see the cream in the carton, and the boutiques in New York say the customer's attitude changes. The milk bottle is likely to remain the drab sign – the economic stamp of the machine aesthetic. Resistance is expected to be wiped off in the tragic-looking disposable early stages, but the spread of cups and plates is considered inevitable.

MUCH OF THIS MEAT IS DOG EXCRETA. The housewife puts her fingers in her mouth. This way may end in blindness.

THE DEADLY PURITANISM OF THE CITY OF NEW YORK IS ENRICHED BY TECHNOLOGICAL INTELLECTUALS COMPIL-ING A HISTORY OF LOVE. The architecture was harder to define: spindly forests muffled in snow.

IN THE UNITED STATES, WHEN A MAN HAS COMMITTED HIS FIRST CRIME, HE IS MOVED TWO BLOCKS, TO PRO-TECT SOCIETY. That means that they have left technology and gone human, and these men have been sent into the state of being XYY.

DON'T FORGET YOUR GENES FOR DARK EYES.

YOU HAVE TO HAVE YOUR FACE PANELS PRESSED, and you learn what shape your face is from the point of view.

WITH POINTED KNIFE CUT MOUTH HALFWAYS AS SHOWN: open for use; closed for protection.

EACH FACE IS DIVIDED INTO OBLONG PANELS which give an impression that the outer plastic panel belongs to an effeminate male. One of the panels lets down like a trapdoor, and in a maximum security hospital anything can be inscribed on the outer panel – a circle or a square. The panels arrive with an additional hinge, and often an immediate change is made. Like a card-house they are assembled; less than one in two thousand is collapsible. The men and women lie side by side, concealing their physical differences, their behavioural prohibitions. As soon as it is light, they display their most striking characteris-tics and other secrets; faster and faster they move, the old men competing with those of much younger age, and the sort of thing for which they are punished is genetic crime. Jokes are made about the link between brain abnormality and style, and some of the style is very white indeed. It must be done by drugs or something self-exploratory – that is quite clear. As far as we can tell, they can never control the symbol, so the treatment is a total waste. After a time there is evident a slight loss of gloss in the personality, from his environment in fact, and various drugs are added. The doctors make various predictions; you can buy their words – they change the signs – fifty guineas is best; it is possible that cash is important – its function is found in the bank, where they keep the best symbols.

WE ARE OFFERING CATS TO EVERYONE TO RELIEVE TEN-SION; a little bit of button is homosexual and happy; happi-ness is a very good product; the law should be nationalized now and then; pancakes at breakfast remind people of the underground; start the day with urine distilled from tea – it will save you from the liberal arts.

another month gone, you know

THE FADED PEOPLE SPECULATE IN THE COMPLICATED SITUATION FOLLOWING THE DEATH OF RELIGION. Divine possibilities follow death: though the bishop burns with death, the urgent martyr is not persecuted. Nothing is happening for a thousand years. Superb communications go straight to heaven; the neon makes a taller cross in the sky, sixty feet high to gape at for hours. "Love your intellect" is practised by the archdeacon. Personality is really Christian; shabby clothes are not baptized; Jesus was crucified and humiliated, as was customary.

THE LOCAL CHURCH WAS ASKING FOR SUBSCRIPTIONS to cut the parish in half. The danger of crossing the road would prevent the people from coming to church. The petitioners have since collected even more solicitors. The old people seemed doubtful; everyone lacked faith in the winter evenings. But the Duke knew exactly; he went back again and again; he was furious. The marvellous man was enormous; he wanted to look at the coats and raincoats; he had the fabulous idea of shopping in shops; he drove down the straight road north. Meanwhile, the retired chief constable was more sensible, and the actual committee of powerful names…

THE DUKE IS A GOOD SINGER; he plays childish games. He agrees to sing a verse with his tongue, as proof of his sincerity. He's not exactly musical, but he's fond of maids listening at the keyhole. Only recently he had been excited. When you're young you need Don Carlos – you've so much energy in the voice. And this maid pouring the yellow wine, which she served her master, he knew to be his. Then the unmusical man is buried in the sand. His hands are presented to the wives of committee members to grasp for a secret purpose. The royal family is a new name for God. The allegory costs £50. Not surprisingly they like to get a member of the royal family in a dishevelled state of undress; they press a thumb against the stranger's ear. The glass tongue in the royal throat is involved in the ordeal; they add a bite to give more pain over the face; banging the head with a stick – the knock makes contact eight times a year. There is nothing after dinner: a drawn-sword dance is given with musical swallowing; the law keeps the ritual going; the dance with daggers is magical; the enthusiastic Duke repels intruders; his hand on the towering masonry gives the sign that is sometimes used as a satisfactory answer; he prepares his equipment to photograph the alcoholic festivities. The distressed widow waits outside with the coffin, her hand closed on the plastic skull. Boys and girls are asked to help by being murdered.

THE SIGNIFICANCE OF THEIR SACRIFICE he saw, as his forefathers did in their time. He visited the town when a boy went to war, and photographed his history. When a girl married, he made the boys march round. There were some who claimed they had seen him running in a circle and saluting, and the girls recalled the inflicted shame as they curtsied. He recorded these events which are visible today and still surviving. The war was remembered in church on Sundays, although it was not pleasant. It seemed to be a town where everybody was as servile as the stabilizing mechanism built into them; the population appeared to possess a surface which forbade collapse by refusing to be cut off from the surrounding area. The Duke would not permit any rapid movement from the rural areas, because of the atrocious roads. The one woman who used to delight him was gone, turning her bottom towards the dead. And now the war had started, the infants were thrown in the river. These bereavements were described in words and pictures for ever. One mother made the photographic detail extremely difficult, because her child had drowned in the pond and she never turned her head without bitterness.

THE FILM is balanced into the sun, of course; the tricky picture is useful to lighten the day. The pleasant shadows speed around the sun; the royal face is made very gentle as the colours change. The bright rim is slow round the auburn outline; the rich colour tends to blue failure; the artificial day gives orange shoulders; the yellow film creates cold eyes; the sunset is for future use as the tree moves farther away before the flash reaches it.

THE YOUNG HAVE BEEN EATING HIM for thirty-seven years. Gazing through binoculars at girls in big beach clothes, the brightest beach of red women; the red-globe golden love; the female slap across the face as the man in the brass cage took pictures.

HIS BEAUTIFUL CANVAS YACHTS are involved in the texture
of royal living – the sloping line of a boat against a wind that
has come wandering from America and the Cape. The con-
cept of an hour; a gale. (The high wind chasing the miles of
sea, blowing the Atlantic into a hole; a murdered man on a
wind-wrecked ship, under the water of the smashed ocean; the
slashed cap turns green.) But I never saw these craft in vicious
waters. He is lucky to have money. Sometimes he collects eggs,
or the birds themselves.

HE PHOTOGRAPHED THE QUEEN, sitting astride her horse
by moonlight, standing in a crater on her personal birthday.
There had been an emergency on the recommendation of
the Prime Minister. The Household Cavalry were to be acti-
vated immediately; the armoured brigade took readings from
strained gauges as she went on: "My troops were pleasing
from the start..." Isn't she elderly? You know that she is. She
appeared to be affected by the glare of sunlight; she came to
rest gently and did not tilt; she was laying the firm foundations
for sound, permanent improvement. She had been in Hansard
several times. She slithered four hundred yards on her belly
before walking into a trap set by security police. "Who suffers
during a period of inflation? Isn't it the Queen? You know that
it is." Owing to the weakening influence of radical politics,
poverty no longer ranked for tax relief. From tax surplus the
twenty-five killed in India's cyclone were to be equipped with
new clothing and a plastic digging device. The emergency
resolution swept the Eastern states. Asked if she would take
into her home two boys trying on new jackets, she replied: "It
is a matter of fear. I am married, with a daughter and a son;
I live in St Paul's Road, Staines. Should I fear Allah? I phone
the police. I phone for the ambulance. I cover the face with my
handkerchief." Eight men, protesting that they were "cooped
up" (their identity was known), had helped to murder with a

0.22 rifle. And cash had been taken from the royal house. Thus the boiled housewife watched her darker masters. She knew she would get food, in case of Russian attack. And when the boy's imprisonment was signalled from across the river and his green pullover disappeared in Vietnam, she was found, passionately lying in her walled garden.

THE END OF NATURE IS IN ENGLAND; the innocent magazines are faded; drowned in money in two years' time.

THE LEADER OF THE HOUSE OF LORDS is happy and fulfilled; he doesn't like plain girls; he has six children. "I feel everyone can become beautiful. The truth is I'm tied to the physical life like Barbra Streisand. I have a mental picture of dolls at the age of seventeen. I don't have to feel them. I know what they're like. Fulfilled or unfulfilled, I find some people terribly romantic. Mrs Kennedy is exactly the same. You should do something creative to express your fantasy. I fix my mind on the plump seventeen – the wicked idea of women. I just sit back, happy I'm not married. I imagine myself close to my three daughters, looking at them being born; the eldest is growing old – I see wrinkles; the feminine thing is terribly pretty; I keep thinking actually that the world is frightfully important. One of the nicest things in the dark is someone to love at a party."

NINETY YEARS AFTER, the statue of Victoria outside the Empire bears no insignia of her own.

THE SCENERY IN LONDON will lead to the glorious society, but saddened by the disembowelled future a hundred gathered for trouble outside a church. A man is placed in front of the world. A loudspeaker released energy. The honoured heroes stood in a circle; anyone can join the nonsense. The sparrow had heard it before. The paper slogan is revolutionary. People dislike the nose and coat; a finger points at something. The answer is faith-healing every Saturday morning. The speaker receives a directive issued by God, but he cannot face ridicule. Jesus travelled overnight to Maida Vale, spent some nights in Fulham. He wanted to know the way to become the most loved person on earth.

THE SUBURBAN CINEMA CHRIST WAS THERE, spending a week in Britain, preaching at the Albert Hall because Billy Graham was in bed with flu. They were boys together; they fell in love; pointing his finger at Mary, going "bang bang, it's war". The spiritual scum led others to the Lord while Billy and Mary spent six months in the States. Then he rang up from Birmingham and asked the people to go on a crusade. He decided he needed an organization in October, professionals to work at it. Billy was looking for businessmen (his chunky cardigan cost four hundred pounds); his relations were scattered round the country, working for the Lord at reduced rate. The Lord told him to marry a young American girl, and he went away on a youth night with Betty Lou and her psychedelic rhythm while his transcendental wife was missing.

THE PARSON IS SPECTACULAR at the age of twenty-five; feeling unconventional, different from other people, because there are books in his house; roaring loudly round the whole town most Saturday afternoons, passionately, during the period of self-doubt. "It's worthwhile once a year keeping in touch with people. Mrs Davey helped me come to Christ." He had a nice car – a wonderful gift. He looks like a lady from the Church. "A man dies, and the funeral at home is handsome, rather a delicate service; a friend and I barge into the room with various people; the wife's face prematurely frightened white – I think that's marvellous. You pray to God for the novelist's ideal, and that includes sex; if you want a bit of ass, that's the advantage of being a bishop."

DOWN IN THE GARDEN THE BISHOP IS FEEDING THE RADI-
CAL THINKING EMANATING FROM HIS FAN-TAIL DOVES.
He admires the gardener, bent with the courage of the people,
trying to make the flowerbeds into the Gospel. Digging it up,
people can understand, the work of some remains in the field,
with the muted elegance of a barrister. "Rich people do the best
work; the early Victorians knew where they stood." Despite
the growth of creeper inside his house, the walls are hung with
new opportunities. £3,000 for the reform of gambling, an
undisclosed figure for the treatment of alcoholics and miscel-
laneous repairs. All the influences make the bishopric sound.
His two uncles think he is a good bishop. "I think my father
was at Eton." With parish tins of Coca-Cola he is repairing
lives. There is no more room for improvement. Both daughters
are pleased. His wife pays the price.

THE BEAUTIFUL BISHOP WAS ONE OF THE FIRST PEOPLE
TO CRAM THREE SECRETARIES INTO ONE DAY – he showed
me two himself – he had one every hour on the half-hour; his
day off each week is spent at the House of Lords. His taste
shows right through the red ceiling; his Persian girl is speaking:
"What's the use of passionate Christians? Very effective; bare
against a wall." "One has a desire for love like raw meat. In
the Christian face the missing teeth are symbols of privilege."

TOTAL STRANGERS PLAY THE PIANO TO MAKE HIM SMILE.
He glanced down, embarrassed by it. "This bit of upbringing
of mine." The munch menu sounded awful if you put it into
words. The bishop's lobster was uninhibited; he had a capacity
for close-knit camaraderie. "Swiss trains are clean, like good
church people." He was preaching something cheaper; he
took the service of England. "It's not just a matter of talking
to the wife, you know" – discussing a clergyman tortured by
the people.

MOST PEOPLE WILL CLAIM TO BE PEOPLE, USUALLY.

THE CHOIR SINGS OF COMMUNISM – half a lovely hymn about a Romanian dean who speaks the language of theological literature. The priests are rational enough, but what they said turned out inconvenient while the political climate is changing.

reason for change	this is bad luck
Britain in front	swap roles
how long?	in Greece
I understand	and now in Zanzibar

THE BRITISH COUNCIL IS A REMARKABLE SURVIVAL OF INTELLIGENT EYES; their action is prescribed by the trim beard. The classical voice knows how many booklets we sell to the gorgeous children of believing families, and the number placed out of sight behind the screen.

AFRICA IS OUT OF LAWFUL REASON. The jungle is allowed to the inhabitants. It offers the maximum wind, which blows and gathers the immense momentum of the years across hundreds of slow and hesitant tortures. There are reasons for the action, and for the reactions to it. Careful information is collected from the muddled nations. Nationalism is advertised under pressure – the sunless hothouse of separate slogans. The motor vehicle is put in prison. The flag flies over the trees.

THE PRIME MINISTER IS UNCERTAIN IN THE SENSE THAT HE WAS TAKEN OVER BY THE ARMY TODAY. The police and terrorists are forming a government. Independence is what you want; in January the war is on here; the liberation will be three weeks ago. Lady reporters patrol the streets; the radio men moved in; neither group wishes to fear the other; the reputation for being terrorists does not last long. "We don't demand release of prisoners." The troops help the existing government to resign for a fortnight. No return to rule is planned.

ECONOMIC OBSCENITY WAS SUPPORTED BY THE PEOPLE; the aim was a few dollars' worth of inflation. The police were certain to win; the army occupied the streets in total silence and steadiness; the minority died of cold.

THE OPPOSITION SUPPORTS THE MOVE. "That's the guy to shoot from the top." His ambition worried them. Everyone was shot on schedule, for successive numbers of hours, with white face staring in the evening, the daylight smashing into the face suffocated with tremendous energy. The brown prime minister stoops in spectacles; shoulders point straight at his rival; now they can see his voice is not questioned. With multi-technical tricks of tightness he survives the battle; he controls the road himself; he bellows his word; he cows the complicated men with his energy and presence.

WITH BLISSFUL SUB-MACHINE GUNS DRAWN IN FREEDOM, seven ministers stood in dreadful white paper. The fortress was fitted with nails; the dungeon sound of public occasion; the trumpets dripping and flat; fireworks floundering. The casualties were promoted, too, by ladies in mournful gaiters – five women specimens of monster: their length and breadth offended. Coloured ribbons were used for decoration by the heroes marching past, the grey-green distant future overhead.

MILITARY AIRCRAFT EMBRACE EACH OTHER. The war dead do not hit back; they are received in soil, riddled with hail.

CAN WE SALVAGE ANYTHING? Is there anything to be learnt?

ROMANTIC MUDDLE, ROMANTIC CREATIVITY. Are we going to survive in some way? Numbers increasing steadily, decade by decade; people are leaking; these are crises. Forgive me, but I do not think that this is even half true – even of the smallest of them, the vehicle of community: the family. Some sort of social and political fragmentation; some sort of dissolution sooner than you anticipate. Families are falling apart, falling away from the natural pattern – the intimate parental relationship.

CHILDREN ARE NOT SUPPOSED TO POSSESS SOULS. Nonetheless, their fondness for someone's face can be unpleasant.

INVITED TO LUNCH WITH HER FATHER on the day of the fresh start, the girl in the home, surrounded by babies: waiting, like the end of a term. On the other hand, when the father of the girl said, "What do you do, then?", surprisingly, she said she liked knitting. She talked like a girl, that is to say. She said she was studying for her O levels when he gave her a good talking to. She had one eye on the television set and one on the baby. And when her father arrived to see his granddaughter he waited for his baby to explain exactly what the position was, her ear cocked for the telephone ring. As he asked her if she was glad the child had been born, he was naturally apprehensive when she said "Could be", and how could he be informed on what concerned her? When he asked to see the baby, she retorted: "Her first sight shall be her own home." Her expression most serious, she could not change, as he could not, and most of the time she did not know who he was. They could not meet. "Would you expect me to look agreeably surprised?" he asked her. In the home he would not leave her alone; she was one of his girls – one of three. She did not like to be called his baby; she wanted to be out, like an appendix is out. He had been using her for a purpose; four weeks ago he had invited her back to his house; she had promised to come at the end of the week, because she knew this would shock him. For a year now she had lived in town; she had taken her stand. Though she missed her favourite pop programmes, she confessed that there were three men involved. "Unfortunately," she added, on a rare occasion, "I'll be away for much longer than that", when her father charged her with having intercourse with them and they were sent to prison. Yet she was not the first girl to have a baby standing in the park, and equally it was not her fault they were sent to prison.

THE GREY LIGHT ON THE LAWN; her relations dreaming in the afternoon; her friends slowly and happily following what was happening to her baby.

THE BABY WAS SICK IN THE GLASS; the awful young was sturdy, pale-coloured; concerned about her teeth she was. Her hand grins and folds her lip; she can't say sorry; her top teeth stuck in food.

PEOPLE LOVE A BABY. Little babies are most painful – they have to be looked at all the time. The woman-child in her behaviour developed despairs; the mother underlies her silence, sitting and stroking her – the exact opposite of her sexual feelings; a highly unpleasant physical sensation.

THE BABY-SITTING BISHOP HAS A FUR HAT; he coughs in the face of the baby; he is working for the first time in his life, blowing the layer of dirt from the wall. "I don't know how people can live in this way," he says hungrily. Holy men must eat. He is plumper than the child.

THE PREGNANT THREE-YEAR-OLD IS HURLED AGAINST THE WALL; a baboon is strapped in a bus; the corpse of a small child shows restraint. A different type of injury is sustained. An unborn baby is better than nothing. The impact breaks a bone. According to the sex of foam rubber the fair passenger with the firm moulding of her outer skin reproduces what happens every night; the flesh is needed for discovering why.

HER BOYFRIEND'S HEART WAS GOING BLUE; he couldn't stop smiling, dieting on fruit in Woolworths. Two policemen in pink shirts sat together, asked him how he'd saved £15. "It's nice to have some guineas around." "We only want to talk to you." With lots of love and other things in his pockets.

A COMPLETELY NEW THEORY OF BREEDING AND IMPROV- ING CHILDREN: a prototype of the high-speed youngster, avoiding the discomfort of a failed education. Radically new humanity needs a four-wheeled drive – a youth-control system with the zigzag child encased in plastic. We should not under- rate them. The lateral oscillations, the minimal aspirations of children at high speed, should improve the youngsters early in their lives. The soup served in schools is stagnant and ineffec- tive; the signal received by the school which has lost its vital tension is proportional to its failure and social inferiority. Machines shorten the future. He talks of libraries in supermar- kets presenting information on cuts of meat. Living industrial processes which customers can cash; the electronic transfer of the child by qualified technicians. Transfer should be orientated towards group acceptability, developed in the future to give fully automatic control. This would need entirely new suburbs with good domestic managers, who would be kept largely separate from the existing system, with jazzed-up hoverpads supported by middle-class invention, with mothers and fathers of similar shape becoming less motivated but inherently capable when told the state of the signals ahead where there might be advan- tages in individual success.

BOYHOOD IS SPENT WITH CONSENTING ADULTS IN PRIVATE IN THE WEST END ON SUNDAY. Life changed at the fall of night; the ugly suits transformed each time; red sweat men, small boys happening.

THE TALL AND SLENDER FORMER NAVAL PERSON, friend of the Duke of Windsor, belies his years. An enthusiast, he sends a cheerful message to his shareholders this morning.

UNTIL THE CORONATION EGG IS KILLED BY WORKMEN, THE GREEN-AND-GOLD SOCIETY WILL SURVIVE. The Vice-Admiral likes boiled sweets; the Duke and Duchess give each other presents; the medieval icon is sold in a shop; the Bond Street shop is closed to the Bolshevik revolution; the ladies of the family look delicious; art has peculiar virtue; the simpler objects are moved about; an ornament costs six shillings.

BLACK SEASCAPE TWELVE THOUSAND POUNDS.

A REPROACH TO ABSTRACT EXPRESSIONISM, Euclidean abyss, I move to the edge, and the edge has a yellow edge. It should have ended where the dark part comes.

HER INTEREST IN ART IS GOING BADLY. She makes visits to London with her brother. "I am always on the lookout for a genius, and in London we found, in fact, a pretty painter in a fashionable jacket."

UNUSED TO WORK, HE WAS SHORT OF TIME. A painter over thirty, he had moved in circles for years. He looked at his brushes and they did not speak; he embraced the sea-mask of the young. He was not prepared to dirty his hands after lunch. At the back of the white canvas the trickle of oil showed like a bomb. His iniquity is in the top price bracket. "Dylan

Thomas was an especially close friend, but business is more my thing." He knew lots of lovely people with very blue eyes bounding everywhere. The soft arms and chest greet everybody with the usual motto; his business was photography at the moment, as the hand went to the brow. The same business, art business; moving around, giving advice, "I don't care what you say, life is good." In the places to which he was taken he would say almost anything provided the results satisfied. In London, for instance, he protested that the room was full of Tudor socks and that really reminded him of old times. He was embarrassing when trailing after the Queen like a commercial traveller; he complained loudly in Chicago for three months. He loved things like that. His reputation was for being pretty silly, though he always said he would be called charming, "after I'm dead".

THE PHOTOGRAPHER LOVED THE PRINCESS well enough to make a perspicacious move: he tied one hand firmly under her chin, to alleviate feelings of guilt. "Taking off her clothes is a moral dilemma, isn't it?" Now she is setting off for St Petersburg, and setting up business in such places as Monte Carlo and Nice, where, it turned out, the shops were not quite good enough.

ON THE RIVIERA, the wolfish tone is rewarded with success each year. The rich live in nylon socks and shirts beyond the dim white bay. The police play football close to the big hotels. The world of art suddenly turns over: the tasteful semi-abstract simply exists in the aimless present, enjoyed for a week by those who discovered it earlier. The sun lovers arrive late; virtue has not anything to do with their lives; these people are subtler and more tempting. The models are looked at and beckoned all night down the obscene pattern of corridors and rooms.

THE PRINCESS DITHERED IN ALL THE EXCITING WAYS: the affluent American bosom in private hands; the new experience; green cuisine in a private garden; the combination of revealing French and Tahiti grey; the pretence of eating a bare man; the clever diet of morsels of meat throughout the year.

TOO INTELLIGENT TO CLAIM SCOTTISH ANCESTRY, she lived with the problem of identity, privately. Coming back on the accelerating train, looking back at the Queen in the north, risking money extremely seriously, she had set foot on the world. The humiliating week did not trouble her much. Whenever she got the chance, she superbly lowered her eyes and saw herself rising in the morning for the service of the world.

IN THE ROOM IN THE CENTRE THEY SOLD SALMON; the pink pool, exquisite with eggs and cream, served with coloured spotlight, played on the arms with cucumber and cream on parts of the body; the different twinkle on the wall; blue and red philosophy joined in the brighter whiter production.

THE DESIGNER IS PAINTED BRIGHT RED where possible; he is gently raised above floor level and placed on a lavish sofa; he is completely spoilt in the centre of the room. His furniture of suede is unlike suede; the suede ceiling is his inspiration. He wears his clothes in his room; an elderly girl strokes him admiringly, "I like to adore him." He numbers his women; he reels off the list. The ladies enjoy his private life; a cup of tea every three years; perhaps a bit different on Tuesday nights; he uses his mother; he invited his mother quite often; she were a right bore.

THE PRINCESS SWITCHED TO HER OSTEOPATH; the devoted blue eyes were dotty, the giggling waiting in the curious room.

"I get up and stand on the carpet. You need to feel vulnerable."
Eating her fish humbly enough.

IN THE CAFÉ WITH GREY MIDNIGHT GLASSES, the customers found fault with the length of the tables. The waitress turned round and tugged at the tablecloth; the coffee turned sour. For two hours the crowd shouted; a police officer questioned the people; the important colonel whose hair was short kept his temper because of his beard. The policeman said he believed his colleagues had a sense of humour: "Every day the bald colonel congratulates me and gives me money." The colonel said the cracked face of the academic type was his favourite political prisoner, while the man with his hair down the street was put on trial for begging. The gentle waitress stayed in the coffee shop till late at night. The colonel said artists were absurd, committees were suspicion centres, and "Money is more beautiful than poets". The minister in charge of the souls of the youth said these sentiments were unacceptable; the colonel had acted without advice; the police should not have acted at all. "The Christian conscience is the first and greatest aim of all old soldiers. Men give their blood this year to the General in good faith. The rising price of lamb is a measure of the value of the nation." An American journalist had caused the trouble. To the police he admitted he was wrong. All children agreed that rising prices were lovable; it was precisely the beards that upset the youth movement dedicated to the regime. The need for clothes was created by communism; few people could avoid giving offence. The Government cancelled the red plot; the demand for meat was bloodthirsty and boring; the details of life were not hygienic; the weirdies wrote circulars against the reds; the Church was without serious faults; the red representatives were unable to run the country; the army did not deprive the army of its pay; the blows on the side of the head did not look so bad.

eeeeeeeeeeeeee
eeeeeeeeeee
eeeeeeeeeee
eeeeeeeeeeeee
eeeeeeeeeee
various problems
of groups who
can help
a letter has been
sent
rapid growth of the move-
  ment
in our minds
too much
if you are set on it
he defined the need
the point is

but surely
surely
we need help
the nature of relief work
is non-political
try if you can
liaise with me
first step is write
letters again is what we do
this is a good time

at Christmas time
you can't do these things
some have done it
teach-ins and debates
combine
the cost

THE MIDDLE-CLASS LUNCH is ordered for visitors; the lean man keeps in tune with an infinitely friendly Indian. The players take time to prepare the game. Famine was the subject of meditation by the gay family in the garden. The spiritual leader's laugh was startling; most people appeared at his lotus feet; thousands thought it natural to respond. "Much as I disapprove of the stock exchange, I do admire the market reports." Booming oil called Yogi; the advertised discussion lasted two years. George Harrison was stained deep maroon, dicing vegetables with surprising vigour. "Some people don't want to sit pleasantly, and somebody ought to be thinking about that." Ladies moved in groups; newspapers described a man with beard and jeans; the woman exposed in glory, her sandalled feet manoeuvring – pale skin, crude film; it was all right, the couple were discussed; she attached herself with the originality of an artist to something foreign, with mood of abandoned humiliation. How many males sat on the brick floor? To teach nothing?

"YOU NEEDED THAT, DID YOU?" "Yes, a sort of pre-death emphasis on sleep."

told die four weeks unless find thousand pounds depriving someone else seems terrible because the choice of live or die unreal the choice stop the respirator leave to chance oh no oh no cannot switch back natural heart perhaps switch off heart will never take off

THE PHILOSOPHER IN HOSPITAL showed signs of an actor's impatience. He began to shoot questions sternly, making use of rifles and pistols: "Are you sure you have studied Marx?" His padded luxury women had phenomenal bottoms; his best friends had waited for a decade, crippled by the stiff-necked male, for him to be crucified by bad treatment during the course of an afternoon. Now he found it difficult to question, over and over again, the heavy bed piled with pillows. He paid money to the hospital staff, expecting to be chucked out for singing insulting songs. They sold him seven nurses with one lavatory each. His lungs depended on the murderous reality of the seven-horsepower petrol engine. The ugly lung was made of iron; it stared heavy with indifference. The shaved head caught in the black scarf smiled daily; the iron tried to imitate the mouth. He kept trying to live in simplicity, to adopt the cult of reason. He wanted to throw the dartboard at the flamboyant bishop, fool enough to comfort him. Steady of hand and drinking to the end, he left three thousand pounds to an anonymous research foundation.

WATCHING PEOPLE DIE IS A VALUABLE EXPERIENCE; the electric disorder in the chest deflects the pen on the graph.

WE STAYED AT HOME LIKE KIDS, in the stretched arm of exhaustion in August. Father had one day left. He asked about his heart. The doctors told him he didn't have one (slicing salami in various ways).

I GAVE THE NAME WHICH I THOUGHT I WAS. She broke the news. They said there were twins and I was the girl. They advised me to write to the Salvation Army for fifteen years. He put his arm round me and said, "Hello Glad."

THE PASTEL-COLOURED ORPHAN looked demure as she reported that there was nothing to it, yet she was muted in the sort of dismal dirty-yellow brick hospital that afternoon; coming downstairs, her heart was shut away. "I'd like you to come and see the piece of cake; it's the kind you see on advertisements; it's on the table in the sitting room." She handed him a plate. The calendar stayed on the wall, and before lunch they had a glass of water while the young mother with the wedding ring described the details. He was asking what brought her to it, from the physical point of view, when the police reported that the muscles were not tightened yet. The boundaries of irony were reached when the father discovered the child hiding under the table, and the naughty girl spent four hours alone in her room before she crept down with hysteria. "A boyfriend twice your age is understandable, but afterwards what did you do?" "I went out and left my baby in the snow." Scribbling in an exercise book the name of her adored one. The matron lifted the baby down, highly coloured teeth clucking scarlet in her blouse, carrying the carry-cot downstairs with messages to Romeo and the Rolling Stones.

VICTORIA ROAD HAD ALL THE GLAMOUR. Outside No. 66, advertising a drinking licence, the electric light bulbs were running round like a dance floor in Rome. Luck gradually turned and changed the place into a popular basement worth five thousand pounds. The owners were rightly proud; the previous owners had not known their business. The dancers thought they were in the sea among the neon lights and patterned flowers and posters that brought a touch of glamour from under the floorboards.

ANONYMOUS LADIES KNOCKED AT THE BOTTOM OF THE ROAD unexpectedly; they arrived over the wall in the back yard; they marked the road with a sign; and soon the car park began to prosper. Others wondered what was happening: "Anyway... I mean... you would... if you had hit him sudden... when everyone was pissed as me..." They jumped on the neon wagon, and everyone had a good time when the signs went up all over; young people in all the rooms; the voices of well-shaped women stuffed with blue.

THE SHOWER IN THE ROOF IS SCALDING THE GROWING GIRLS. The flexible bottom is happiest. Anal control is cheaper, and can be used in the seven different positions, though expertise is needed.

who kept him talking downstairs while I was born in Battersea; he just pulled the mattress back across the bed; I did not like to think about the head and shoulders with legs landing in the bedroom; I dealt with the girl cut off by the bottom of the bed, but at that time Barbara said "Cor dear, I couldn't move – I just lay there", and we didn't even know there had been one; I wouldn't like to meet that one; I couldn't say I saw him go; somehow nobody thought; they were very much a happy couple; one had read a book – she had imagination; I got to know her later on; I was too busy working to get involved; I should have been working Sunday when she ran into the room; I couldn't afford it at the time and now I'm not living in opulence; it was in August; it was snowing; there was this woman living in sweat in this room; the flats were converted; I got home at one o'clock; the upstairs flat believed in ghosts; the house retained its turrets; and I walked in and there she was, shaking, on the Monday Barbara left, and I'm a bit worried that she'll come back along the tree-lined drive like a nervous leaf. I could get her back by telling everyone, and this is what I'd say, "All right, Mrs Martwell? Have you seen a ghost?" She said he was living in her room; it was white, no eyes or mouth; I thought it must be Barbara, who lived in the three-room flat on the first floor, until she showed me exactly where she saw it the second time, when she got up and put on her imagined things. Nobody was told that when they rented the two-room flat; while she kept walking round the bed, with glasses on to get a better look, she had a laugh like no one, not even her mother; but the flat on the same floor was where nothing, of course, had really

THE EXACT OOF OF THE HIDEOUS THUMP
(exultant thump)
The bride cried in fright
Uncomfortable in her mind
Went very quietly with the officer to the Swedish ship

THE CLOCK STRUCK TWO DEAD. There were trees overrun with dead ground, with the statue of a hotel; a patch of dead shaken with comfort. Two young women rediscovered vegetables, the shape and taste of a pear.

THE WOMAN WHO DIED WITH ALL THOSE EARRINGS ON, her father owned a helmet that would break a wall; he thought he would lean on her neck with the helmet and make her die; he was fearless till he was seventy – when he closed that winter – she could not believe it had happened in London as fast as that. Spring came and she touched the wall with her lips, talking continuously in public – this was the thing that caused her spinal injury – the terrific pressure for three years hitting the spine at the top; killed by a fallacy that happened on top of her, the right side over the left side, she knew she would not swing back again – she had to be strong, but she was growing old overnight, one leg left out in the rain; agony with boys across her path; she showed the strain when her arm was set; something grew out of the wood when she smiled and went away against the wall.

IN THE WOOD: NOTHING BUT HOPE, later on destroyed by polluted water which lay in the quiet hollow. The dark pond suffered most, confident beneath the surface – grim size it was, long, smoking, huge eyes covered with green slime; no doubt sewage weighed yellow – industrial yellow; sold to escape the inevitable. The deep had been left so long undisturbed – it grew worse and we had no heritage. The big brown cold came, and the long canal was a sad place. Those streams of green will soon be thousands of pounds when he has died years ago under the weight of trying.

WITH AN URGENCY BEGINNING IN DEPTH, the sun's rays got down to where the underwater grip no longer penetrated. Samples of water showed rich plankton pouring into the sea; the chemical navy floated on the surface; the population of slime had broken down; the food nutrients could not spring up. The artificial nations brought aquanauts to analyse the pools. The continents germinated; the theories multiplied. The shallow seas illuminated new fish; the scientists added to the area revealed. The pinch of horror was felt under observation; starvation showed signs of being choked down; empty stomachs the size of Africa going staring mad in the face. Speaking of financial matters: light up the seas and watch the distinguished explorer suspended for one hundred hours in darkness thick with particles of fish; experimental seaweed in the house for fishermen to catch; goats in a steel ball for seven years gradually stifled; investigating manganese and gold.

HOW ESTIMATE THE COST OF WATER? The sea costs sixty-five million. The sea is softened by marriage with pure water, but nature practises thirst in a way that allows water to become a triumph. Huge tracts of rain are bottled for sale in London; they sell the surface concentration of energy in salt, and in this focus of nations in one place, a thousand miles of land in the north are brought to disaster. The savage sea has many tastes; the corrosive attack on the kidneys; strangulation by rock. With little rainfall, or several ounces, roughly fifty million tons is too much as the day drenches the North-West. There is no scientific attempt to emulate distillation, for seawater is the source of fresh water; the process is developing; the nations need salt water, and, after all, the water instantly vaporizes. He can foresee the time when all those people will live in deserts where the water flashes into steam, and they themselves need him to tap the oceans of water for life. Nature parts water a number of times in succession, by simple methods, from stage to stage, at a rate, and at a price.

THE TRUTH IS there is a ritual and skill in earning money, but consciousness begins and ends.

IN THE DAMP CAPITAL OF REJUVENATED MEN who make money work, beauty earns money on the King's Road. Sex is sold from a slot by extremely tough women in out-of-date clothes. The paper skirt is a napkin splashed with pop colours; foreigners are interested in the powerless city; the dress designers argue for a dollar; the increasingly mobile children make life easier.

THE CABINET IS RULED BY THE BUREAUCRATIC MOUS-TACHE. The Government manoeuvres without dignity; several ministers have insufficient sleep; three hundred guardsmen keep the roads clean; their silk helmets amuse the inhabitants silently. A dark number of officers drink whisky with agile boys; their job is to peel potatoes. The locomotive is considered a great joke; the driver is expected to kneel on the ground; the passengers are carried round a roundabout and each has kisses prepared for him. A narrow shout is heard from the females stretched on trestle tables whose red fingers are curiously shaped.

WE BUY THEM IN LONDON – DIFFERENT SHAPES OF MOUS-TACHE – but we don't want them here, dumped in the parlour, painted in yellow stripes to make the people happy.

THE STREET IS AFLOAT; the mild voice of the moustachi-oed director-general on the platform; all are committed to a weekend awash with free wigs and wild publicity. The technical excitement of attempting to swindle the people came over strongly, especially the unbuttoned cheque books with enough power to launch an aircraft against the elements.

THE PUBLICITY ALONE WOULD OUTSHINE LAST WEEK'S EPIC, but no one knew how many would pay for the fun of playing soldiers. The high hopes were anchored when neon signs were banned at night. The skilled man-hours jostled to be last to take the risk in the interests of progress. £100 a day, asking and getting the story of the wives, and a few others who'd been missing for three days.

THE STREET PHOTOGRAPHER IN A DOUBLE BED, eating chips magnificently on the second day of the season. He slept like a thousand pounds; he did not seem to be accompanied by relatives; he was eight thousand friends with everyone; he had five teeth to speak of; he slept in a stranger's room for two weekends; and he put the question: "Which side do you want to know the colour of?"

WHY SHOULD ONE EVER RISE FROM A LONG SEA JOURNEY? No individual decides in fear of his neighbour to save up for the long journey.

TO THE CATHEDRAL WALLS COME MEN IN RED BECAUSE CHRIST'S BLOOD AND HEART ARE THERE – in the chapel where men and guns enact tragedies, beneath the church. The blood is preserved in the place; in the building he died; the flames died; the word will make them pause. The men for weeks called themselves modern; their error was modern; the old lessons were analysed and elaborated; the crucial experience found between the museum and the tomb. The modern men were fortified by war; the refusal of existence. The famous war was based on the facts of life; the paper conclusion reinforced with concrete. The truth remained in the cellars.

THE ARMOUR-PLATED CATHEDRAL was built in retrospect. Twenty thousand aloetic and cactaceous plants were replaced by a cathedral armed with tons of TNT. The church is a strange place, with machine guns in the afternoon. The child is three thousand years old and made of straw; fingers of plaster embroidered with blood. Cathedral arose on the basis of organization, fifty tons of DDT, the sword of faith, plenty of planning, half a million anti-malaria tablets on an epic scale. The initial scheme was cathedral-warship-orphanage – three in one. Then the military moved in; the war was a hardness in a dry time; the soldiers flocked out there; the tombs were mobbed for a short, uncertain season.

THE CROSS AND NAILS ARE THE FOUNDATIONS OF SOCI-ETY. Even in London the war helmet is honoured by bishops and magistrates. Jesus was a rich man surrounded by soldiers. The army makes Sunday a holiday. They maintain the normal pattern of slavery in the mines.

THE MOSAIC FLOORS had climbed the shaky dark, and the hands in front banged into two eyes in front of him. The reflectors threw light towards the cathedral windows, sliding up and down into the darkness; the coloured windows winding over the iron floor. The walls were caught in the copper light and the priest could be felt listening for the signal from the choir. The weights, the drums, the organ sounds unwound like lust dragging a ladder through the air; steel ribbons leaping like a bell-rope in a tower; the heavy bible shivering in his hand. The signal bell fell twice, bellowing down easily. The caged dark settled itself; the bell came down to give warning sound again as the people travelled into the void. From clouds of unsafe omens, feeling towards the white-lit door beyond the warmth, the priest ran towards the group arriving. "They don't need me here – not for any sort of job." The voice behind the darkness talked for a minute. "No," he was told. The walls were padlocked to the iron stove, the oven packed with coal on the floor; Christ's blood danced on the ceiling in the heated chapel ringing with men; the noisy virgin with split bosom and buttocks took her fun at the wall and nobody noticed when her cunt exploded with someone else. The wall of stone laughed louder, shaking the bed, swallowing gin in the hope of the new morality, while a wave of thoughts bore into the bone of his shoulder for a moment in the maze of saints in the rows of tombs below the clouds of glass. The signals in his throat slid down and felt cold; the iron hook divided the vertical planking; the foot fixed by a nail, rotten with netting on the farther side; there was the man whose eyes advised him clumsily, holding him, preventing him from falling into his bowels in the pit; stunned, lost, calmed, he dropped without touching the terrified beams.

THE VOLCANIC RESPONSIBILITY FOR THE CUP IN HIS HAND continuously for nine hours. Unparalleled violence ahead. Immediately the memory erupted. He could see no witness. The priest got out fast. He could see the interior of heaven for four and a half hours. Asleep on the outline of water, he had been climbing the night, with mixtures of gas on the way down, his knees returning. The bishop ordered the man back to town. The priest was determined not to. The following day was raining frustration. He refused to continue. The gas was the danger, hacking his way to God and beyond that.

WHOSE BISHOP HAD WRITTEN BOOKS CALLED HOPE, BECAUSE HE WANTED TO RANK FOURTH IN THE CHURCH. He studied science, biology, politics, religion. He said he would be first in the hierarchy through personality. He will be the new kind that has gone to church without religion, without tradition. The bishop believes in London; he might go there for a change; he is so clever. He speaks of his transformation into a saint; his new tie is tied in knots; he is consecrated, concentrated, unlikely to make allowances; he doesn't think it unkind to be accurate. His Anglican relationship grabs the headlines; the popular controversialist has written about his attitude to his listeners; he has digested them. He is an explorer himself (though at times a stiff upholder of the tight circle), a philosopher and a shooter at life. God comes easiest to those in authority. His mathematics sets the river ablaze. He keeps money in the corner of his room.

THE BISHOP IS SWAYED BY THE ADVANTAGE TO RELIGION as he prays for the soul. Known for his love of gifts of gold and silver, he specialized in furs. They are seen together – vestments and furs – smelling of incense and shame. "We are judged by our jewellery." He chooses a ring of value, followed by diamond rings; he complains he has no platinum cufflinks, "I don't get more than one a month." His corsets are part of his vocation; a piece of silver was a famous symbol; wedding rings come into his mouth, the diamond eye cashing it. "Far more educational than pictures", they told of "knowledge and love of the past" and "all the usual costs have risen".

THE BISHOP CANNOT LIVE WITHOUT HIS ACCOUNT-ANTS WITH HIM. He has twelve. There is no problem they cannot solve. He has paintings of religion; he believes that God is sound and light. In the swimming pool he stays with a quiet nun for thirty-six hours. He built a house for God nearby – it has two beds, a medieval piano and other statuary. "The Roman Catholic Church is my country that made me rich." He is free; he has a child by either wife – one is the "son of a friend". The child is sustained by an electricity socket most of the time; its father is a human female – a photographer of great kindness. Now it is too late for him to travel a lot; the flight to Cambodia is too expensive, though for years his wife made love in the plane. "The free man must have somewhere to hang himself. I have my church; my religion has many rooms, hundreds of preoccupations, ten thousand songs. God is Napoleon with flats for his staff, stuffed with Greeks. He does impersonations, makes jokes against Himself. He speaks to people with kindness when He has time. He belongs to the public. He cannot be a really bad man."

THE BEGINNING WAS A RIGIDLY RESPECTABLE SORT OF BOW, a wave of things, until one of them turned overwhelmingly religious in front of everyone and said, "I don't want organized church-going – the people tend to hold the hand of the Pope; he gets upset easily; he must go home to bed." They had chosen for their modern church a striped and lightweight minister. Their rendezvous was known locally as "on the other side". He held that the church was at the crossroads; it should have a slightly modern look. The priest held the hand of a fat woman in pale blue; the congregation kept racing off to the notorious "strip", where women from brothels wept with stones in their hands, covered with trampled dust; the gambling bishop beside her breasts as they grew, arching them up in play, where the easy boozers glittered and shouted at the girl dancing in the street. A few girls got arrested and screamed through the night, walking home in the morning, singing about freedom. They had trickles of blood on their old brick apartment houses and they were led by Jimmy Anderson, the long and narrow Negro, the man aware of his words, his marble head on a pole.

THE RIOT POLICE had a remarkable car. It was a block away when the police department who show restraint when a call goes out rushed the girl to Jimmy Anderson's. A large Negro section of men started out for hospital as she lay in bed with a detective from Puerto Rico. One of the poorest got killed by a fire truck; they walked thin in the fourth area; their rooms filled with people as the order went out in the shocked voice of the Negro detective, who partitioned an area of the big floor space among the apartment blocks close to the water where the few ripples made waves as he tried to hold her hand. The notice over the door said "HOMICIDE FRONT". They had their place in there; the police controlled it; they had to stand there as the officer fired a little pistol at the girl's sex, with aggravated assault. Naturally they had to take whatever the cops threw at them; they shot her as she fell near Anderson – the tall man, older than his considerable amount of action, going under instead of going in and arresting the floor. Instead he made everybody in the store a partner of Groscinski, and they understood what he meant. The ringleaders were eleven policemen, who were told to stand still and keep quiet. A tall member of one squad was a lieutenant; five others had the action covered by the district attorney's right to give notice to quit right there because he was dark-skinned; the duty sergeant and fifty detectives owned squad cars and by special order were allowed to use force with a blue shirt and white buttons. They handled on the average one homicide with one car assigned to the particular Mike Canaletto. The Chief grew a new moustache every two days of the year. "Violence, Marianette?" said the detective. "Them are called smoking guns; these problems are crimes that come out of the pathos of the human condition, because murder is still a trend plotted by detectives in their heads." Tragedy: the head kind of opened and fell to the floor, then her daddy came to the scene or was known to be close to headquarters. There they were marking up on maps the numbers of millions of immigrants when the bullet took the cable out of her heart. Others talked of mysteries with coloured pins from all over the world, and they stood still, and her mouth clamped shut and the doe couldn't open it, and this was comparatively rare. Some police force cars were manned by maniacs, but most of them were struggling detectives from the burglary unit in the gruesome routine of their work, patrolmen in civilian clothes in the least desirable section of town. The girl's father and both men were almost casual; their coats were plain fawn; waiting in the city to get a foothold on life, they seemed composed. "What kind of messiness is death?" Agitators are instantly recognizable by the police – almost one third of the total have no hair. "Did you notice his hair?" The cops are not too nice to them in their vehicles; the big chrome spotlight is on the Negro; crime is about to be detected. They are soon dragged into the front passenger seat, and the police have a duty to attend with suits and briefcases ready for autopsies at the morgue; white eyes and whispery spectacles; ballpoints in gunbelts; a big yellow wallet for the client. Shrinking into side streets in groups of three, one was killed by lack of care. Police organization is being perpetually straightened by letting them work against the incidence of alien cultures. Would you know the policeman if you saw him in a nightclub studying the crime sadistics he is thinking of encouraging for statistical convenience? I think I would.

CASSIUS CLAY was summoned by radio police: his house had been ransacked by ministry officials. The boy with bare knees had attacked the man-made menace of the air-force officers. Then a rifle had been found on his floor. "I was going ten miles for a pigeon shoot. It was not to murder or kill." Cash had been seized in his house. He was accused of acting as courier for the Russians; he had been paid £80,000 for five Turkish divisions; he had broken into the home of Lord Cornwallis and stolen works of art. He said he was travelling to a new job in Adelaide: "I am pleasing from the start. I can win by-elections. I can win municipal elections. People like me at the start, but see the end results." He had been talking too long to expect to be taken seriously. He too had been in Hansard several times. Seated in prison; his blue head; a monk without furniture; the unusual words he tried to understand. His last chance to speak had come in this building. The strong interpreter turned to convict; the forced answer contradicted the first occasion; the clear answers tangled desperately; the ruined skull disappeared; the room became upset; the human form destroyed by hatred.

THE PATTERN OF PROPERTY INSULTS WAR VICTIMS. The attitude is clear. While they put stones on graves the army is in Ethiopia, the anarchists are destroyed by antique insects, the price of food is fifty pounds. Lunacy for ten minutes makes its gesture; the poor use public libraries; the pianist dies in the war; the property remains. Teachers are tortured to death; businessmen remember that cookers with frills inside are big earners; seventeen million puppies buy petrol on a winter morning; the gallons are interested in politics. The TV birth rate continues to rise; the elderly faces are frozen; people have refrigerators in a multi-racial community. *The Times* is engrossed in modernization; the power station shuts at four; the final notice has been undeniably effective.

THE SMALL COUNTRY with the impossible standard of living. The dirt grenades are Chinese. Trucks are revolutionaries. Groups of children are shot without resentment. Life was hard. Most of the men stood side by side in small houses.

IMAGINE THE DIVIDED COUNTRY; thousand-mile-an-hour speed limit – disguised motor cars rip around everywhere. The place is white and two-thirds coloured; a strange place two days away; not too sure where the war is, though street signs tell them. They killed natives with a shovel; the Texan general arranged everything. The happy life was plenty to drink; the rain was taken for granted. He is one of these people lazing around; peasants live like waves as well – they draw a veil over labour, they depend on the slow tide.

THE DEEP JUNGLE REJECTED THE AMERICAN GENERAL who went sailing with varying degrees of force into scores of disasters. Victories were disasters; he was a man to shoot communists; the story started in ancient times. At pistol point on foreign soil; the General who was drunk changed his mind. He drank a couple of thousand whiskies, guarded by riflemen who shot dice. The winnings paid for military disappointment; the forests lost the last of the war; the roads were as bad as in London; the up-to-date American weapons missed by an inch. The army has its own reward: recently the fighting is over. This part of the jungle was living a million years ago; a horse stumbled over a shell; and rumours of the quiet rebellion were murmured everywhere. Single grenade thrown from a wall. The military base is sited over a landmine. Two hundred men smudged the shape of the foreign smile with green food; the wooden plate on their dinner table was very fine; the guns were raw; the mortar bombs weighed sixty pounds; a hundred and seventy families felt like people who had lost more than others.

PATROL BEGINS SQUARE IN THE CHEST. Flare makes the sand white. A man can see his feet through the village. Dog crouches in trash, a can in the hand stops his jaw. Twenty booby traps go silent. The physical end of the mother consisted of contact with a modern American rifle.

my fingers found the painful missile
1969   with my blood xxxxxxxxx in place at last
ambulance driver
wax tableau
kill him
everything grows from war nightmare
x   vx   x   v   v
second   I extend my hands again

                                mickey mouse
                                minnie mouse
                                two sweeps of steel

        see
        what I see   time   h
        a young   time   o
        xxxxxxxxxxxx   time   r
        mister   time   r
                                                   o
                                                   r
        _____
        scrutiny   time   h
                                                   o
_____   r
last swoop of love   time   r
no matter how filthy or ugly her   time   was   o
        I should have a visored cap   r
AB   in this space I smelled resin
ME
        the
        shot
        which
skinny
        shot
cold here

NEWSPAPERS CONTAIN THE SPIRITS OF DEAD PEOPLE. History has all happened and doesn't matter any more. Geography and history have a running track circling round them. The radiogram proves that nothing is an emergency. After the battle of bits and pieces, watch the piles of stones: the Celts killed strangers cruelly in the gloomy morning; the long worms see their dead when killers are about. The spiritualist radio dabbles in life in the scullery where the use of water is forbidden. The tropical torpedo express train goes cold at eighty miles an hour. The garbled message is brought back dead.

GENERAL WESTMORELAND WAS SEEN AT THE SPRING SHOW OF THE ROYAL HORTICULTURAL SOCIETY YESTERDAY. Heavy bombers again pounded the open rock garden, the valley area, especially the primulas. A variety of weapons, for example, showing superbly flowered specimens, while troops were moving towards the Botanical Gardens...

DEATH ON DIFFICULT TERRAIN (during the monsoon rains the authorities do nothing about the mud); heavy American finger; whispy Chinese guided by peasant. The fat General smelled the soldiers' brothel; the poor place was forgotten; the characters followed one life together; the missing child was denied existence. Whisky in one cubicle was a game to play; the married were regarded as renegade. The General fought for the unmarried daughter, with a week's pay from the United States four times a year. "When you walk with the commander-in-chief you're twenty feet high." But the girls were changing fast; the ancient film cautiously showed them the sex life of soldiers with no restriction on their movements. The passion of Chinese girls was very welcome; the serious soldier was rare; the beauty from the good family was guided by her ancestors.

I'M TERRIFIED OF FLYING DOLLS. I torture very young people with machine guns; they get knocked down for licking my face; my eyes fall out of the sky; I've been a cradled child for two years; I've had women in the most difficult situations – they lie down with a couple of guys, I lie down – it's very exclusive; I saw a man one morning full of earth, face covered; one made me laugh; the festooned tree of madness; a custom I understand; the broad back gave cover; there was a threat; the dead lie down and think in Asia behind a curtain; candle-burning stars left out all night; a dirty off-white body afraid of the sound in the chest.

THE BLOATING AND DEFORMATION ARE INSANE. A striking and disquieting child, she ceases to be charming. Naked female body depends on feeling close, like a pet. Woman's body might envelop a sizeable lifetime. Suckling babes or lovers are curious in extremes. The beauty of hesitation. Quaint doings in wombs. Objectionable mess, paste of white, associated with depressing vegetation. Men prefer women coated with mud, disguised as pies. Add piss to a tin of mud (the value of piss). Paint with mud made fluid, slightly wet. I prefer a blonde across a table.

WITH MUD ON HER BIKINI SHE DANCED ON AN ARMY BADGE, standing outside the kitchen done up in fluorescent rayon, tempting the boys to follow her into one of the bars; wrapped in a leather jacket, walking round the stage, some of the guys intrude on the girl doing her bit; sitting over her, they take off the tops of their uniforms; the hottest girl sits with them, a nestful of moneyed Americans, in one particular café where passers-by join hands and talk at you for a beer; dollar notes are fifty cents each; driving through every doorway, enjoying chilli sauce with hot pickled vegetables, eating bags of walnuts at a hundred miles an hour, the sincere man says "love you" and the boy whose legs are bad wears his open shirt in high places; the best lays are elongated women in the centre of town; a girl sails out with soldiers naturally; she strips from table to table; soon she's wearing white; slowly the girls are brought back and the throaty man says they're back; bikini's on her way, and when she strips off, her brothers are waiting for the spectacle.

THE GIRL SHOUTED IMMEDIATELY, excessively high. Her ambition was to live modestly, but for the troops she was not pliant enough. Her mind ceased; her conventional thought was a knife in sensitive areas.

THE TALKATIVE GROUP AGREED ON THE NATURE OF WAR.

NO BREAD.

LOAD THE PLANE WITH BOMBS.

SOMEONE STARED AT THE WOMAN like a rabbit looking beneath a skirt. On that incoherent morning, the rain gently destroyed the fire; it was nowhere. But the chin was broken. She was caught and tried to scramble, screamed and floundered, threatened to yell, choked, said nothing. Some stared at the bomb dropped in the street, the swinging shock of explosion for thirty hours, teeth like dominoes laughing, the sun smashed on the road face down as the slam of a shutter. The fall dulled the pain in the arm, kissed the horse's ears feebly; the broken knee talked nonsense about a bomb, the leg against the tongue in the shaking room shaped like a bundle. The light came from tears which supposed companionship and fell into oblivion. When the eyes opened again to crawl between the closed eyes, the light was too hot, the cracks in the head remained and struggled towards each other. The face rusted into private misery, pulled forwards, stroking it. Out of the smiling kettle floating before the staring torch, the steam surprised him. The face in the blanket made noises. I thought I saw the left arm out of order, and it seemed to be, I could not be certain; I followed it to one side, with bread in my hand. The body was in good order; it could run a few yards; the pain casually stopped. I offered food on a comfortless handkerchief – lucky egg on dark blue. Brutality touched their eyes; one after the other raised his head to look into the sky.

TO ESTABLISH CONTACT she stood there, now dead, after the skirt had been raised above her head, because the face meant the dribble at the corner of her mouth, I think it meant the mouth of a dummy, the face thus clothed, female muttering, metamorphosed mother, the boy holding her hand; the family would be in the bag she carried, navel cord wrapped round her throat.

HER EYES MADE A WOUND; they were filled with dark; she located him, digested him. For this reason he continued to bleed for a long time; he looked for her and could not find her. He had good reason to suspect her existence, her proximity; he had good evidence.

ON INTIMATE TERMS WITH HER, the memory zigzagging downwards, not yet a person, taking biscuits from the dead, from the corpse of a shot dog, making a mechanical night of it, the boy is made to walk in his Sunday best; noisily in movement, the heavy burial feels friendly; others gather round; they offer him bonbons, herring, stopped her protest with earth.

HUMANITY IS STRONGEST WHEN IT TEARS YOUR SUIT. Would you like me to be a communist too?

ASK THE FUSILIERS. The flat I had there was beautiful. But these people here, they show resentment against the army. I think they are barmy. We work very hard; you might not see us working. But there is a potential for riots. We are forced to respond. We deserve help. Bayonet is a symbol: of family help.

USE THE BONES OF A DOG as a hunting device. The poor dress as a dog to increase strength.

THEY SWEPT DOWN to dynamite the famous tank. For hours a day they hid there, in the long dark galloping with its long guns, as they cut the veins of the young captain.

THEY WERE HALTED ON THEIR WAY. He fired shots. "They are my friends" – pointing at them. If we paralyse the city, the bread shops will remain closed. He confirmed that his men made decisions concerning weapons. Fired two shots at a helicopter carrying. Asked for and received assurances. He ordered the hand grenades to be thrown. The second lieutenant ran. Fired six or seven shots. Cutting the officer down.

THE MEN WHO DYNAMITE THE TANK MAKE THEIR OWN COFFIN. They plant explosive in a hole in the ground. They gauge exactly the thickness of the crust of the earth. An error of three or four inches will blow you to pieces.

UNABLE TO GIVE THE NAMES OF THOSE INVOLVED.

THE NEED TO KILL WITHOUT EXPRESSION. What have you to say about war? He said today it is a necessity, though here the country unhappily is often sub-human.

IRRESPONSIBLE BUDDHISTS, hooligans and communists, inscrutable Buddhists, fanatical Buddhists, shaven-headed, hot-eyed, student-cum-hooligan-cum-communist, suicidal Buddhist frenzy, suicidal Buddhist fanatics, juvenile riff-raff, teenage hooligans, Buddhist extremists, fanatical-suicidal-communist-orientated Buddhists riding high, wide and ugly on a wave of hoodlum teenagers and communist-paid fanatics.

YOU HEAR POLYPHONY? On either side the sun performs without anaesthetic. Through the jungle blue 3,000 dreams are playing games with a long pole; the bearded child goes into action; wriggling fish are dumped in the mouth; mutilated mushrooms in an iron pot; twenty-four steps towards salvation. Society lives in mud; the water is not boiled; Stalin is the logical conclusion. The round-bottom builds her house; the son of God is an army officer; father wrapped in a blanket listens to the talk of frogs.

THE SOLDIERS IN THE NARROW STREETS kept the people away. The chief of police was paid for his part in the physical murder. The widow shouted at the centuries. The major pointed angrily. The symphony orchestra vanished. The major smiled on the phone.

THE TOWNS AND VILLAGES APPEAR TO BE SPLITTING. There are signs of rebellion. Important persons and papers are strewing money in influential places.

AFTER NINE MONTHS' WAR THEY DO NOT BELIEVE IN BATTLE. Several young men have given up the idea of honour.

THE YOUNG SOLDIER was basically ordinary. His life had been hard labour. The girlfriend was difficult to obtain. Others arranged for him to go into a world in which he could "survive". The uncommon Negro had an American name; his departure was glamorized. In Vietnam he proceeded north – a deliberate act of immorality. He spent six months on humanitarian grounds. He was strangely affected for nearly a year.

HE CONTINUED UNTIL KILLED DOWN IN THE DARK BY MACHINE GUNS.

A YOUNG MAN RESEMBLES AN INSIGNIFICANT STREET ON HIS DEATHBED, the same when he is ill. The exhausted face has no connection with the plump child. His father was a butcher, with the same badge of office; the son had a red carnation at four and a half, and a hand dipping into the chocolates. The boy in sickness is half in and half out of tragedy. The man is looking at the fourteenth century. And so is the river, telling you something two years later. With him, the bleak land died.

OUR CHILDREN KNOW THAT EARTH IS DEATH – it offers the chance to stand at ten to three. This is what narrative events could not do. The round is seen looking at the world. The bullets have glory angles; they understand the kill. The body works like a newspaper illustration, striking the dead lying on their own. The brave learn from the gesture of doing it now; he learns from words who has not words; the light expands or diminishes it. You can do nothing but watch the reconstruction of the past; the face of reality dips his dreaming hand in dye; the future will not come out of the cupboard. But words are heard through the hive of glass and the paper sculptor does the rest: twenty chisels sharpened by fire, red points in the air. "It is possible to record the family in the garden in the afternoon, or as a vision in the evening. But I expose them to the day. Compare them with other men's faces. Get the terror in the face. Induce sickness by determination. Fix the effect of those who die. When the mind grows tired show the exciting results of drifting faster than words. You can steal the action from the next man's identity, and make a collection of someone else's words." This trick led him to the light. He fitted beauty into a wooden box by making glass boxes coated with paper in bright sunlight. Hours were needed to force the glass to print and fix the pattern onto paper. Round the walls of the narrow evening the room would not stop talking; the magic possessed the light, and all that nonsense.

THE ROOM WAS FILLED WITH HEAVY AFTERNOONS AND EVENINGS. It helped to be among nice people, nice furniture – a wardrobe belonging to a friend who had gone back to plumbing when he made the grade. A better job was what he wanted. He had a house, he had a car, sometimes, at night, a small scarred table beside the window. A packet of tea was his habit. He visited a young lady who seemed to realize that unlike everybody else he was not going away. But his form of heating was not good. And when he lost the gas, she moved out. She could not make the grade after a few weeks of that. The bulb was hitched over the bed; his place was in bed with the light on; maybe there would be a crowd in the drunken house, shouting in the centre of the ceiling, walking round the house again at two in the morning. A well-educated man takes time to get a job; he went back again to try the police, but they had gone. At that moment he could not see a way; he wrote to his family and said he didn't want them to see how he lived; he did not like the pressure. It was like when he first arrived – now he could not get out of it. He slept late, then he did not lie in bed any more. He was frightened of sitting in a chair, tried avoiding loneliness in bed, listening to trouble on the radio, pulling himself out, because he could not climb out.

A GOOD PLUMBER IS A THEORIST WHO KNOWS PRECISELY WHAT IS HAPPENING.

HIS TWO COATS WERE CLEANED when the weather was good. He took the bus and leant out and looked: the weather was bad. His cap and trousers smelt in the bus; he came home to his nephews. Halfway back the cracked boots walked home to the old house. Fivepence was found in a locked drawer; the money was washed in a tub and left for six hours; he put the halfpennies in the bank. The small man read the papers and left them outside once a day. The leg lurched to the doctors when he moved; the ordinary man looked after himself. The local children had no money; a face went back behind the door when he died in the crowd. His house by his own standards was already stones; the man lived on his own. The bitter gate had no visitors; his money inside the house was his own. He had no ability or any other gift. His food was regular; he enjoyed the bag of bones at eleven in the morning. He woke early in the living room; the parcel of coal on the rug. Three panes of glass were a threat to his independence: he blocked them with board. He could do without a jug of milk; the tea he kept to himself. The postman was a human being, an animal intruder: he pretended he was deaf, refused the contact. The social worker would greet him while he was still alive; the hot meal for so long kept him warm, scraping the uneaten newspaper each night; the last chip in the brown bag saved. The hole in the stairs, the hole he had cut in the back, was filled with nails. He held down the cat till it died. The garden grew into the back room, the white loaf went green, the visitor arrived at irregular intervals. He was allowed a reduction in the old-age pension on condition he died.

THE TRAMP COLLAPSED onto the shrinking plate; the meal was eaten elsewhere mournfully under the clerical gaze. The bishop's tone of even texture became more true after dinner, the artificial flavour uncompromisingly modern. The cathedral had a budget to work on; the lawns must be kept smooth; there would need to be room for more cars; we must put the poor on a trolley; watch out for the poor – they talk a lot; we must try harder to be friendly. The bishop himself examines how the place is run; he could not be friendlier; he is exacting; he sees the room in the morning; he kneels on the floor to get it into perspective. "With these people stick to the simple rules: provide them with food and drink. If the tea is moist and the breakfast sticks to the plate, they will not ask for more tea. Let your man have an apple in the cold – a place like this cannot always be warm" – as he retired to the lounge, where he attended to his devotions.

THE CARPETING IS DARK BLUE, DOING THINGS TO THE SITTING ROOM. The curtain of apricot is indulgent. He buys a lot of old records. The formal upstairs room has more than a hundred chairs, an irresistible Gauguin for the first time in the lounge. The formal clock is made of paper. The idea is for the clergy to enjoy what they are doing: they spend a lot of time in the bath. The clerical executive has a face, a book and a job. He was trained for ten days in four stages; he calls himself executive for money. He enjoys his home; he would attract a wife – he will get one; his business gives him satisfaction. He plays golf, amazed by holes, fits in the occasional game with a good secretary.

BLACK DOTS IN SPARE ROOMS. The sound which fits the bathroom is electric tone. The tapestry is interesting. His teeth made a red spot on the piano. The collection of random notes had different names. Growing up is trying. The sound of the past seems dead. The childish lights are flying full of old music. The crosses on the piano crawl across his face. The grown moustache is dining at eight and will not admit he has changed.

IN THE HOUSE WITH THE NEW ROOF, THE BEAUTY DOLLAR FASCINATES. The private room for writing is used in the morning; the bedroom where the long newspapers sleep, the uncomfortable huge room where the guest in bed is moved onto the long table. There is also in the house a hall called

Ceremonial, the pink fish along the glass corridor, the guest in the garden, more rooms, more walls. The marble chef has been removed for grilling the bridal cake. Families have parties on the balcony next door.

we should make really
tremendous effort
who actually
does the asking?
you would not ask for
money
from Scandinavian coun-
tries
foundations for example
the Christian Council is
trying to send a new pair
of socks
we certainly have it in mind
groups have independence
if you can get the money
no not now
when I was in Rhodesia
what was happening was

this is bad luck
within a month or two
we don't know
it may be a long time
we are working all the time

to release people

what he says about
being attacked in the streets
is true
when I wrote
we have been
constantly in touch with
United Nations
we would make
words
the basis of help

THE SWINGING DIPLOMATISTS in the evening consume their lying officials. The local women find them afterwards, cold on the banks of the Thames. When they have friends, it is either where the river begins to narrow or in the homes of foreigners. The sticky cakes are quite romantic; the quiet old liqueurs cut the throat; their charm is astronomic. Their exotic dinners are served by window cleaners and black-dressed baby-minders in the triangular marketplace. Ripe fruit is rare; the sun shines four miles south; the chic little shops washed down by rain make the pram-pushing girls turn grey. The archbishop broods peacefully in the eighteenth-century bookshop, wearing his entire traditional costume, with attendant women exposing the knee. The display is organized by the clerical service to glamorize the aristocracy. The park is full of police successfully maintaining the law; the flourishing culture of introverted women serves the needs of the rich. The fringe of professional hair becomes an island; the good reputation is impossible to find; the streets are choked with trousers, as they wash their lawns single-mindedly.

ALMOST EVERYTHING WORKS WITH CHRISTIAN MODERN TELEVISION. A friction if you need it, you lover of peace, though, of course, "Go out and buy it." A viewer pays taxes on human beings; anti-communist he certainly is, and he wants everything that a human-animal-lover, a joiner-of-associations, could possibly want. There is no quality he does not possess; there is nothing but that which may be possessed. He has the personality of Indian toys and vodka; he is everything from Finland; he is costume jewellery, faceless and flabby; shrunk heads are the formulae which decorate his mantelpiece; an imitation phallus made from pressed-out plastic, sculpture too light for its bulk, brassieres engraved with hearts, imported camel saddles, experimental goods for consumption per square foot; television messages inexhaustibly obscured by the incessantly alternating image, the slogans which existed at the time of my youth, anything to avoid the rush hour, the express change and credo of the road that runs beneath the family man in major cities, the man of property who seeks the substance that remains. On weather-faded crutches (foam rubber will seduce him) the other will carry his crippled master. He will stay in the suburbs; newsagent and confectioner, the utterly forgotten rusty pram, the child will sigh at the sight of the window pane; discomfort still exists, the worn-out generation is not easy to find.

THE CITY BELONGS TO THE GO AND GET IT. The bread of the rich enters heaven unerringly.

THE PRETTY WAITRESS FROM THE SPIRITUALIST CHURCH began with the vast eyes of a woman in love, and the seven nights a week were in her heart, handing out endless happiness. Home is relaxed and jiggling with milk bottles. The morning is shared beneath the window; the left arms of stragglers dance on their hips, speaking of helmets and sizzling chestnuts, frost spilling over a field.

SHE HAS ENGLISH EARS. The swinging young understand an advantage of this kind. For her, London was middle-aged; like men and women, love and death were nasty words. Something bad happens when your body is naked; the French have no modesty; the risky Latin brings new rhythm; Lolita in bed has Anglo-Saxon eyes. The surprising experience unwraps the masculine voice; the workman in blue elastic hugs the gutter; his words are a game that goes on all the time. "Anyway, it's nice to be freckled and gentle, to make a perfect little whole for oneself; best of all, at half-past three, vigorously, with strong wrists, till the pain shows, wash your hair, that must be very hot and very smooth and very clean and absolutely dry."

THE THOUGHT WAS BORN IN THE SPACE between the bed and the wall, the wall holding the lamp on the other side of those years, looking backwards. The years had been hard enough, shaken by crying, lived in rigour.

TIME TO WAKE. The man slept. The girl laughed in the kitchen. The hand sprang from the shoulders. The ritual razor at the mouth cut the nostril out; he cut his face. The smell of the day at the door again, thick yellow smile, damp bed. He ate love, the egg across the table, pepper lips; people were not in their room; trees on either side of the earth, their heads touching, curved body escaping, hands hot in the house. The Homburg hat stepped into the room, thick friendly men, rich fish. The bed in the second room, the place of business; the girl knew nothing. "When I give her these." Fifty photographs of girls and money – he was pleased to make money from the house. He made her hold herself at six o'clock on holiday this summer. The place, the sheets of green, in half an hour: her body in his room; the distance to the mouth; the mirror above the bed. He had loved before. The edge of the bed, legs between sheets, paper money in envelope, girl with comb, the comb tangled the red hair; she had her paper toy, red coat. The door answered her question. There were fifteen chairs and tables in the house; a platform supported her bed; the room had two windows. He lifted her body; his nails hurt her; the quick pain touched her; she could not call out. He heard her cool voice, the mood altered; she did not know it. She had ceased to live years before.

HE IS DEFINITELY IN ENGLAND. I sleep with him each night. He was in hospital in Belgium. He may still be alive. As a balance to these hopes. He has been seen, both in this country and in Europe, without official confirmation.

I THINK I LOVE EVERY THREE YEARS SINCE 1938, a couple of weeks before Christmas. Certain natural things are constant. The heat and the sea. Who was it who said? The smell in the nostrils is not unpleasant: heavy containers of hot meals. Beds and sheets, white and clean. And there are bicycles, collars, memories. For me these places are unchanged. Four hundred miles north: sausages, baked beans, Irish stew surrounded by greens. I saw two monkeys for many reasons shouting their messages non-stop, and of course I knew they were saying something else. You can smoke, you can take a room, though in that room I never had a good meal, the plates and walls all gold and red. It's only a small town: winding the clocks is work for a month; you see a rat in your bed. The girls are quite unusual along the main street; wonderful green and blue before sunset. When the lights go off she has to like you. The admiral is lost among the famous ladies of the town.

NO ONE KNOWS TIME like a street girl – she goes by nothing much more than a bell. With their flowers these girls have the pride of passengers on the last train of the night. From the outskirts, going to the West End, what they have to offer passes slowly, studied coldly under the clock. Theatre-goers at night give the girls a lift because they are there; a woman, then two more passengers, squeezing benefits from need. The drops of sweat on the thigh open their short coats with heavy sighs and smells. They need a scarf round head and neck. There are more than thirty tumbling sisters on benches, with rows of others talking late, but there will be nearly seventy men waiting bleakly – not sure why they are there, for people don't offer a bed at the start. The last business of the night lies draughtily between anemones. She shuffles up in preference, for an hour cramped in trust, the dress drawn over her eyes, her lips moving above knee level. Dozens of fellows walk beneath a poster at dawn, without tolerable purpose.

THE HOT AND HAPPY THREW STONES which hit the patches of grass in the normal pattern of the town. The frightened woman realized how brave she was, proving to herself that she could save money by living near the iron railway, bent in the anonymity of the sea of suburbs at night. She reached her home in the shower of stones slowly out of the dark and turned left into the avenue where the boys threw pebbles in the dust. Her nimbleness was not impressive, but it was light, and she could dodge the bullets. She bent her arms double to make them look strong. In her teeth she concealed gold money. Lorries crowded with Irish shotguns loaded with lead carried her along, bulldozing churches on each side of the street in hostile territory. They walked her with them as the crowd refused to move, synagogues tumbling down the broad street, the grey-faced shock threatening like a cloud on the sun, when the shouting started. Machine guns mounted transparent churches with classical obscenities, in a litter of lenses and films of royalty the technique of shots was feared and hated. Bayonets pressed the middle-class town, seized and dragged a girl over the horizon. Under the bridge they beat her on the easy breast worth less than paper, the heavy oval dressed in sweat, her hair wrapped round her heart, high and rounded white outside the shirt; down the street unleashing love, the pretty girls followed with shame in white, dozens of flimsy hearts bent together, almost together, one of them weeping in blue, the sombre elderly huddled ugly while the football racing young men controlled the dangerous place.

A CHINESE STRUCK IN THE FACE BY A CHAIR had a cut on his face. He refused five men; they frightened him when they came – they started smashing, and several Chinese lanterns were destroyed. The blade pierced the left arm raised to defend.

THE BLUE POLICE LIGHT FLASHING was danger to the blazing boys. Like bees and minicab drivers, they swarmed downstairs. Oil-stove through the window, others milling around with pillows and blankets from the crowded house. The heat built another fire quickly in the building. They found a man dangling, stressing the terrible disaster, in the city designed to have no fire.

PACKAGES OF NOTES were loaded into a lorry. "I didn't mean to kill the copper." Police believe the intruder is still wearing roller skates.

THE COPS CAME SKIPPING IN HERE, looking for a fight. I was chatting with these butterflies – the room had several – screwed to my shoes. I'm in bed, on layers of old carpets and rugs which my father didn't wear, and by seven the floor was looking pale with sheets of Perspex. The doctor in a dark suit asked if I was ready to go, because my chest had been known to fail. "Do you ever have trouble with your boots and socks?" They probed the condition of my brain. I found that lengths of plaster made good clothes; my hands joined together to stop them knocking. I examined my jockstrap in the lavatory; I had to study it before I could get started in the business. When I was overweight I cleaned my trousers with toothpaste in the kitchen and left them drying in the boiler room for two hours. Marlene gave me a hard hug, but I did not acknowledge it, from shyness, as I finished dressing. Finding my watch or car key at this time took me thirty hours, while Marlene said my day was empty. So I spooned more sugar into her, with a nose-inhaler. All sorts of possibilities in tubes were opening up with this pretty long-haired blonde. In an afternoon crowded with nervous managers she'd say, "Everybody's hobby is running for trains." She relaxed a little when tired through hunger. The junky actress had sausage and mash for dinner. She cost £21 for the night, or the equivalent in steak and mushrooms. She went to bed with a sauce bottle – she had a stock of eight – she was one of those people who dream of them. But probably not tonight, all the time whispering "God Is Good, Jimmy"; she had Vaseline behind the bone, which almost blocked the passage where the sweat flies up. Tired and half asleep, her husband has nothing to lose. The pair of dark spectators had fed-up expressions and gave little whistling grunts inside the room.

THIS FRIDAY MORNING there will be another murder. It will happen in the kitchen. Throughout the afternoon they watch the pretty wife killed, the long moan from the throat, licking her body; there is no reaction – the people have committed suicide. In our homes the crime is talked about; twelve policemen yield $3,000 profit; there is a note of the fact in their journal.

BILL AND KITTY HAD A GOOD LAUGH ON THE TOP FLOOR. They would not come down. The wife sat quiet at night, and I imagined her halfway down the stairs, or taking off her shoes in the bath with the water running over. When I went up to the top landing, there was never anyone there, only the *Woman's Own* on the fire, the smell of burnt paper in the room. Her husband at the back woke up when I was there one night, and that night pieces of ceiling came down and rested at the bottom of the bed, and Kitty got up and did the Lambeth Walk on the side near the window – it was there we had more laughs than anywhere. Her husband was a radio engineer in a food factory, till he washed his hands of her. On his head you could see the hair that used to be there. For two years she had been trying to get rid of it. His head had hair till the rain completely devoured it, and what remained fell into the street. For eight years their home was a hard place for her, and when they moved it was down the road with council officials taking the furniture away. They had never seen anything so funny; it was a funny business. "Derelict?" Bill said "So what?" Their child was not even born; they had no surnames, no bell on the front door, six years ago. Their baby was born in the back yard, where the little body was found with eight shillings in the cot.

WHEN ALLOCATING DWELLINGS they were always walking past the children playing in passages; the smile is frightened; eligibility, in the official view, is three in their own flat if you don't touch them. They stick the children with a woman who lived at the back; the neighbours worried so much; the dreadful place was soon evident – the whole family explained the physical disturbances by the woman upstairs (the clean door does not mean I love it); the little girl is not as bad as that.

MOST PARENTS TALK TO THEIR CHILDREN USING THIRTY DIFFERENT PHRASES SPOKEN MONOTONOUSLY. Educated verbal parents have a grammatical structure. Baby will feed her doll, then boys as well as dolls. Complexities of consciousness, the earlier pivot is underground. Baby boys look for a dolly they can mount. Many adults are able to do this with a doggie, because they have practised with children. They use dolls early on. In Russia it is a good sign when a child grasps a doll. Even butterflies educate baby, their wing utterances in higher colour, deliberate labels, spots and stripes. Daddy barely copes with foreign words a twenty-month-old could understand; speed patterns increase the length of the baby's lip, teaching him to use dirty words more accurately.

A FAMILY OF SEVEN CHILDREN lives for years in a council house. The father is selling them for personal reasons. He gambles on a price of £250,000. Other children are being offered by Knight, Frank and Rutley, the agents for the wife. The remaining thirteen are undernourished and dirty. The father beats the boy who was not sold some time ago. The last four boys are living in the fifteenth century. The price of a girl of eleven is £84.

TWENTY TENANTS who had not paid the rent found their melting apartments unrecognizable in the falling building. Their small brick homes with policemen at the door, the blue lawns moved because of their colour. There were several reasons why the demolition date was fixed for so many years; the time was kept secret from the driving crowd of women. The police found the widow in the violent room, and six who refused to move the following morning. They felt sorry for those defeated men

– the bad people thrown from the window – the comfortable furniture broken in the home.

THE REGULATIONS DEMAND TWENTY-FOOT COUNCIL OFFICERS IN MASTER BEDROOMS OR IN BEDROOMS ON TOP OF EACH OTHER. Narrow corridors strangle idealistic and progressive projects. Front doors are essential. The Norwegians produce pots of paint for £1,000. The country areas are packed with houses, high-quality bathtubs installed in one room create pandemonium at weekends. The builders are playing with our living habits. The weekend skiers need not be consulted about ingenious space-saving sleeping on the floor. The alternative is ribbon development. The garden is guaranteed without soil. The solution to the tricky problem of integrating trees is an owl-less wall. Karl Kaspar enjoys his open-air kitchen facing a road of communal doors. The English are apt to glance and grimace at each other, yet privacy is not for nostalgic reasons, it is merely that the peasant house is not accepted by the public.

THE SMALL TOWN WAITED OUTSIDE. When I returned I ran high on stilts with loyalty to the particular house. The warm stone house is handsome, but every house is handsome. The central heating takes your breath away. After being on the road for years with those other travellers, I faced the long wall of rooted people who could not understand why a few weeks' visit was sufficient. I held my glass and watched the grey community blush when I told them about my five years on my own, as the white chunks of ice in their glasses melted quietly. The ice met the ice, penetrated the house. They invited me to complete the pattern of the thing somewhere else. I explained what I had to do. I would not be invited back. I thought I would feel bored sometimes, but I had exciting things to do. The attractive English girl, the physical excitement in the intense cold, the glare of the river. Once she approached me after she had been walking in the snow. The wonderful freshness of her education that morning, the air in her throat… I had forgotten – I didn't know what to say. She too had been away for some time; she got up early and told me how dry the air was in England when she graduated. I had forgotten that there was no need to worry or look at the trees; I told her she reflected the bread left out at night on the kitchen table – I thought this was a new way of telling her to come back. But I forgot the water; it was hot and sticky; I felt her thin dry fingers touch mine, and I said goodbye to the hotel for a long time. I was caught driving at a hundred and sixty through an open cemetery, with the trees so tall the dead were delighted. And when the squirrels couldn't see the cars, I said we'd meet again, stripped to the waist and moving along the road in October. She didn't believe it – she said she'd known painters mostly, in St John's Wood, where the leaves were far more colourful; she had to get home before dark. Her lips were like ripe strawberries; her hair had some blue in it; her head shook among the green sentimentality. She was in a position to earn real money.

THE PUBLICITY VALUE OF ORANGE LIPS. The fast actress is quite depressed. Her hair is a piece of coloured machinery, red on the days of racing, following the season for money. She is planning to enter the big money, the international concentration of Hollywood cash – £1,000 a day indulging my love.

TWO THINGS MADE HER FAMOUS: never having been seen dancing and never having set foot in America. She compressed within her time with easy grace. When news reached her of her past, being one day read in the papers, she never contradicted any story. She appeared to make her life consistent with her past. Being in the company of men from her home town, she lived in a hotel room with a man older than herself. Though she married the Dutchman, her preference was for the beautiful days of her life with her soldier husband.

NAKED, with the additional aptness of a dark, windowless interior; typical luxury, bathing her mood like a slave whose physical allure was capable, relaxed, contemplative, the picture of erotic economy, exciting despite the ruthless contrast of her technique; the honey-coloured hair dominated the white sheets; the restriction of the curtain made her a victim of tent-like embroidery; the single spurt of her lover of the heavy globes of gold water falling like a quick gasp warm around her neck and arms; after a silence of conscious wine the woman was more than naked; the ice vision exploded softly with ermine and ivory hand, the water falling beside her in the room with other people; her limbs were faintly mad, titillating, frankly, the ordinary women sprawling on the floor, the erotic properties of a rich garden, the blown fruit of a wilful body burning in an extraordinary way, teasing in answer to the call of a deliberate dream, emphasizing the scent of the past, to have some contact with the bed she is indulging her own life, the lines of the city on the curved body, the natural strand of metal placed round the breasts, the lover of globes of gold, the artificial peacock on the carpet; extravagant clothes, her neck and arms, the daylight actuality of the porcelain dream.

HE PACED FOR A FEW MINUTES AROUND THE WHITE PERIPHERY. The tubular detail watched intently. An empty set has walls and floor. This provides possibilities. There were no chairs. There was a box. What there is is noted down. Make sure of the desk painted brown. The money is placed around the woman, an emotional thing which nobody notices. The hunched and sexy sunlight is raised to the critical point of invisibility; the music is absolute. The self-effacing darling settles into melancholy, aware of the leggy girls assembled quietly in the tropical discotheque caustically labelled "Heaven". The cream shirt lies over the chair; the passing fancy munches an apple; the pale-brown people seem less natural; the cameraman descends from heaven to the girls on the schizophrenic set. Art is shuttered throughout. The flapping sheeting is stabilized. The place is empty. The girls fold themselves into beautiful young people who are going to be shot tomorrow. Their postures are velvet. Everybody knows what they will need, but they are sitting talking round the room. In the evening the bored groups without talk, fighting to waste the good idea. Fashion goes with moving, and now he is talking with energy to stupid people in the café where the girl says personal relationships are so important. Emotions will grow more certain, concentrating intensely sooner or later, but this is the party where everybody is deaf and they get more feeble; they say the same thing. "I want a decent flat, but where?" The girls discuss their hair, sprawling on the aluminium bed – very interesting, the new morality, but not action. The aristocracy looks at the year of the young: "I do not really like the youth, but then, when death comes…" The great museum scares them.

TALL DEAD MEN IN THE WEST END seems inconceivable. The stranger who died has gone away now.

THE DOCTOR DOING HEART RESEARCH is successful, because people like being rinsed inky-blue after months of boredom.

HE REMOVED THE LUNG IN NEW YORK.

THE DAMAGED HEART WATCHED THE WAY IN. The medicine barrier breaks down. The injection arrived. The shape of the heart; the foreign substance invades the area; Kasparak was suspected of medical susceptibility; the question blocked the way out of the body; the short-lived minutes did well for a time in the body for six hours. The doctors detected enough to survive the ordinary. Unmarked, undisturbed, he was bombarded by diagnosis of intolerable change.

"IT WAS NOT TRUE TO SAY NOTHING HAD BEEN DONE – we sprayed foam over the burning heart; it was a miracle about what happens to the body."

THE NUMBER OF TOMBSTONES – as far apart as Japan and Turkestan. Enough to hurt the soul.

MANKIND HOPEFULLY LOOKS FOR ALTERNATIVES. 700,000 possible alternatives worth paying for. The concrete train is green. Paris is a disused monastery. Solitude is roses. The wonder of thought diminishes. The light fades in the complex interaction of insurmountable cupboards.

PEOPLE, USUALLY PROFESSORS, big particle accelerators, have grown by more than the factor of one hundred. The decision to build this or that is a strategic decision dependent on the weather. Today is a little steamy, humidly warm.

RESEARCH INTO GLUE teaches that typewriters can be taught to teach. All available buildings, like the British Museum, are to be dissected to fit the new methods.

TRADITIONAL EYES AND EARS have a sense of touch and infinite electronic patience. Materials with names like muscles hesitate to try automatic learning. The appropriate tone of the fully computerized voice gets sterner; the book has taste and smell; the do-it-now information moves fast. The most expensive go wrong often. Gradually the impact of the picture is sputnik-shocked; each typewriter is like a long boring bicycle. The old wear earphones to test the new American picture; any number of minor brains are packaged for the market. The latest computer points to the dog and forms a giant. When asked to do something about it, the child does with a pen; the patient voice expresses concern. The striped people are simple gadgets built for experiments; they push the button marked "America" and their developing doubts are suffocated logically. Miniature power is expensive, but scrambled peanuts in cheaper classrooms will soon be available. The size of the dollar equips five continents, putting together diverse classes, with people and masters arranged in pairs or in groups.

THE SUPERSONIC PARADOX creates chaotic survivors. Poverty is being built. The anti-American car is unthinkable. There are facilities for the child to learn love for money. Frozen food is the start of the bigger car. With high-pressure advertising he sips wine early in the street of addicted children. The very young will grow up to drink from a flask at atomic research centres. The impressive number and poor quality of cars is one thing; second-class domestic appliances are another imposed upon the European nation. The English do not need more space in the crowded university; education is free to harness the power of the sea three years after the boy fills in a form. The Americans spend half as much again: the big manager remarks that the Government dotes on him. State-owned statistics come fresh or tinned; the cancer advertisement follows the law; a few people drop off the line; prolonged suicide is expected naturally to expend itself one day in seven. The suicide pill is sent through the post office. Vietnam is always being worked out. The chaotic intelligent read the leftish weekly for the elite who are non-political. The obscene Americans have money; the straight and personal nut is on TV; Parliament is fitted into slots; freedom is too flowery; only the girls are real when so many things are wrong. The well-paid writer agrees the final figures; the free wife comes in monthly dollops; sex fantastic is accepted as an instrument of state. The girls rely on trade guarantees and in controversial moments produce a polite suppository. Because she is not a virgin, the younger girl will be obliged to use the telephone, while the physically violent woman advertises on cheap notepaper: Six-guinea syphilis, the western disease.

GIRLS AS RICH AS COWS, SELECTED NAKED — we have photographed them before, like the cereals shown on page twenty. She is established in your house. She is best, lean; thousands recognize her uniqueness. She is fed on fish and left alone. Her breasts may be pointed or rounded; they may be naked; they are there for you to use, six times a day for a few days. It depends on your conscience. Remember the sloppy breast of milk in a dozen colours; I wish she were more serious. As one little girl said: "At what age do you acquire your bosom?" "Any time after ten – there are a few signs – girls are different; they vary. A lot are growing after ten years and three months, which is nice. Another group may develop with maturity – this raises important questions, because after about three months they know they will be plagued by bouncing for years: they must be ample. They feed themselves double for growing breasts; the body weight of mother warmth is irreplaceable. Thousands of town girls have been taught by mum. The clean, slightly older girl will slide into a woolly coat. Hours of love-play help development; I have seen them protect their limbs, their underparts. When they grow less shy, they command high prices.

THE MASSAGE PARLOUR IN THE NEWSPAPER OFFICE HAS ITS SHARE OF LEFT-WING ANIMALS — untidy men with no weapons, apart from eight-inch implements. Highly political men are breaking the peace. The whitewashed telephone is broken. There are crowds of spies in department stores. Sandbags at night and doors of sliding steel when tension produces a bomb on the tracks. The Eastern Police make an arrest. You will be protected in the building.

THE PRESIDENTIAL PHOTOGRAPH fell with the noise of glass spinning rain on the panes. The prisoner's head thumped in the bath; the electric lamp appeared in the middle of the ceiling; the electrode buried in the skin. The hot weight fell, dull iron, faint sound; the jaw of a cat, cold in his ear; the valve between the inner and outer ear insulated from shock; we hold history; the limp cat tied with rope, the hissing ceased; the size of the earth observed no change. He had not bothered with his sandwiches. The cat's body exposed the jaw; the wound below the head, blue flower, face in air, regular sound of sun, fibres of metal paralysed, down the broad way, metal dust, rubber honey, tubes, seeds, paper, dust.

ANIMAL opened its eyes. The heat was asleep at one o'clock in a stone bath. The slow cold moisture from the floor of the jail.

THE METAL constantly forced into a torture frame as he dreamt; arrivals forced the doors; everyone said no. Stretching to touch the opposite side, pressing the wounded leg to the door, he heard the voice of a man he knew. The prisoner's indistinct underclothes were moist against each other in the cellar, and no one minded how long he had been unconscious. The voice in the doorway felt in his pockets for half an hour, his fingers asleep. The voice stooped in his ear with white-faced questions that followed all night; his feet over a bridge did not reply, and he felt the pain in his arm tell the truth. A flared match showed a small cut in the neck; the dim feeling as the hand brought the point of a knife against the flesh.

THE RETIRED POLICEMAN PERCHED ON HIS STOOL. His manner was blank indifference. The gush of blood from the neck was very funny, really. He would not worship anything. He had too much chin. He would not burn to death. But he had the dead look in the eye – stereotyped and shocking.

THE PRISONER raised his hand; the insects were taking over, colonizing the Virgin Mary, ambushing the white telephone, doing tremendous damage to her ear; the big teeth smiled at the wires hung on the wall; the man with white clothes put his hand to his chin.

AAAAAAAAAAAAAA	your earlier mouths
Hanoi	you have to spend money
extreme left-wing	reduce the number of
non-violent?	prisoners
no name	within the group
never stop	torn to pieces
we	to mention
been arrested in a round up	what has been
excuse to repress and silence	going on in Greece
pressure from abroad	hit us hard
weeks afterwards	emotionally
the shooting	I think we have
hero	done a great deal
in touch with us	the figures are
released	terrifying
we have not been able to	do
say	anything

THE RADIO KEEPS FALLING APART; the life-insurance man snaps in two; we don't want war in June; the bored and confused shadows of an army dying of poison of the foot; the stretch of land moved slowly; the land began ten foot thick; the sun travelled at night; the physical problem of history traversed the broken storm across the seas; the personal red line of blood was featureless for three years. The war tax is witness to the casualty figures; the heart ends in the neck.

THE COMMUNIST NECK crumbled coldly, hoping. The chemical cloud was devised to hide what had happened. The confused day was final. Seven million comrades returned to join those who lived in danger; the thickening cloud in North Vietnam followed, searched out the moist feet far down the road. Kicking the noise of the guns, the rain was lame, soaking the three or four others – one carried by men, the lost communist supported by a rope. Breaking his arm in two, the other tied by them, holding his heels uselessly, the arm received a cut, continuous struggling anger below. Few were what they seemed to be. The invaders took a road, and another and another, and reached another bridge and another road, and it was not the finish.

TRAPPED IN VIETNAM, the wife's head crinkled green. The name of the murderer stayed on the cross, imprinted in black, coming straight at you, warning you never to attempt to describe the hideous dead which had been there for a very long time.

CROP DESTRUCTION. C.B.W. Law of war. Kinds and degrees of violence. You can defeat your enemy. Lethal. Allow you. Decide ahead of time. You have other types. Attack the mind. Paralysis, type of thing. Discuss in detail. In Geneva, 1925. Britain's own, in Wiltshire. Smokes are thus preferred. Burning eyes. Within seconds. Soldiers driven mad. Both were hurt. They have found eighty pounds of C.S. Riot Control. We took away a grey powder. Mask of plastic. That is, C.S. He observed lethal effects. Report of secret industry. Many died. Skin blisters. Asphyxiation.

WILD FLOWERS BEGAN IN THE WAR.

THE LONG GRASS in the evening spoke of smoke, the undergrowing thinner sack illuminated the distant potato; the prickly

feet appeared in leaves; the floating ice threw expanding blanc-
mange that you could touch.

THE YELLOW-BROWN SKIN OF THE RAILWAY TRACK: river
of peaches; I went down the river of boredom to see the upside-
down trees, and after passing through towns with smoke, going
across country, now I am getting nearer; another patch I've
seen before; I can see the advantages of colour; the trees thick
with people. It was important that in the summer of 1949,
when I graduated, I left that country where the sun caught
them colours like the local coloured paper, and a few days
later I knew I hadn't a chance, when the coloured scenery got
its picture in the paper. I sailed around, but it did not excite
me to pass my driving test; I couldn't understand why I was
made to feel exceptional; I wondered why a racing car should
make me want to go to Europe with twenty-five other young
men! I saw that the trees looked fine in the distance; carbon
copies of years earlier when they had looked better than any
other. As I drove along, things became harder; I began to
come close; I could see the leaves fade behind the house with
servants; I decided to go back. All this splash of the town left
behind and faded out with relatives who were later to die as I
was having another look. It was the colour that belonged to
death; it was pleasant for a while to be back with the mortician's art – far more interesting than this good country where
novelty began to wear thin. I was more touched by something
splendid in April – my mother recalled the old feelings of
dullness when people drove downriver, seeing local people
in the sitting rooms of their houses, and isolation returned.
All I wanted was to see the end of winter merging with the
breakup of the family. She said get out, and I did. A few more
years to see things elsewhere. I got the sense of being back in
second-hand England. Again the nostalgia for the lived-in,
drab, wooden community.

THE ENGLISH EASTWARD CALM WAS BLUE; the boys at school seemed in summer where cricket was playing Chopin's E Flat Polonaise, and the lake curved on a different scale too. There the upper half of the sun broke over and over, loudly on the horizon westwards to the forests' tall and bristly haircuts each evening to play illicitly with the magnolia air. Protected against winter they walked in blue, like smaller stones closed in soil. The sheep is deaf, with impaired speech; goats in the care of nuns can feed themselves. The stone neighbours envy the full stomach; the school is overawed by stone; the big man is a great delight. The country house will move slowly; the headmaster has children; the white fur coat will walk around the garden. Acres of stretched orchards and jackets of apple trees stood to applaud the smoke in autumn; the energies of these months in sunshine, their clear hot shoes filled with apple wine. The shrewd captain from the Crimean War met the heavy, thick-soled farmer marching round the seasonal fields. Living in winter had taught him why the yeast was stolen from the kitchen.

IN THE LONG DISTANCE THE BOY OF FOURTEEN SHOT A BIRD – the kind he had seen drawn at the top of a pole. He brushed aside the sound of school, shooting at the English air. Now in the sky the target moved; his ability changes with the wind; the strength of the sun did not matter. The boy barely murmurs; the paralysed wings are shot; their broken feathers are refinements that distract. The boy knows the regulations, shooting with care and discipline.

WHEN THE CHILD VISITED LONDON, SHE SPENT THE DAY INSIDE A DEAD TREE; she lit a lamp inside the box at the age of twelve. When she left the house she cried when she remembered the chair she had burnt with a match. At lunch her father had a hole in his side; the factory worker was covered with sores; the family helped the husband when he put down his tools to keep his hands warm in winter. Sometimes he stayed away from work to make decorations on the sides of a box, thinking a man was a piece of wood in a particular shape.

THE MANUAL LABOURER SANG IN THE CHOIR for the last ten years of his life; he gained a reputation; he was thanked by the church – "We can't forget that song" – then he turned against his own and was put in a mental hospital, where he decided to become a monk.

I NEVER KNEW THE MAN. I understand he actually lived; he worked in his own way, allowed no curve – it had to be clean at the edge. In a sense he knew what was there: he was there; he was illustrating an emotion. The problem was physical – fetishes, images, objects. "Personality is (a question of) form. I want to do it with nothing (that old standby) to have sailed (stretched) so far and not fallen." His courage was automatic; he didn't escape; he acted through his fears. Offered a head still breathing: "Were this your head I would draw it." The bone dictated the line.

HE WAS BORN IN OVERCROWDED SUFFERING SOCIETY FILLED WITH NAMES. With himself, central to his thinking, art was good, men evil. This recurring theme – art against evil – he saw figures conscious of themselves in time of crisis; he drew them with the energy of a prophet.

HISTORY WAS TOO TRAGIC. Dostoevsky was an absurd experience in a disused basement organized by students publicly thrown out of college in 1962.

THE GENIUS THREW SCRIBBLES ACROSS A PAGE. Increasingly fragmentary construction is a solitary occupation. The accidental imagination passionately battles; the blind man guides the black ink on silk; the desperate man is a work of art.

JAMES JOYCE IS A FAMILY BUSINESS. The people have heard of him. Ulysses takes a taxi back from where he was going.

THE TRANQUILLIZING DRUGS CARRIED A RED-PAINTED NOTICE: We cause the dawn in the deep water. Killed instantly by fatal damage to stop the man moving, the unexpected collapse is caused by flooding; the anger blew up; psychiatric patients ran down the main street and ripped through the fuel store with absolute madness; the houses and bungalows were shattered, the patients hit by flying glass; the continuous treatment involved thousands of tons of gravel across the roads with blast and fire; the damage occurred progressively; cars were up to the axles in boulders; this secondary effect intensified rapidly; something should have been done three weeks before the doors came flying across the street and other disorders.

THE ASYLUM WORD IS SWEPT AWAY. The psychiatric shudder is different today. Anxiety behind doors for years involves a magistrate; the human patient takes a turn for the worse. Repetitive jobs make wild men sane; the Hollerith machine leads to executive suicide. The glamorous parachutist tries to kill the service chief; the suspicious and insecure have no particular love for the Queen.

I CAME OUT FOR THE WAR, but stayed for the funeral of a friend, carrying a basin for a man in a cemetery; he had harmony; a boy was struck by a stone; it lay thinking; it had become real – real beginning, it gave the name of people; it made a dent in the grass.

THE MORTICIAN AT HOME SURROUNDS HIMSELF WITH SKULLS, because he longs for slain enemies. He leaves the wall of granite to rot; the fragments of bone are decorated. The sun tips behind a black rabbit; the grass is seized by an owl; the skinned yellow-eyed dead inhabit the grave of grass ten feet away. Hawks stand on the works of man. They hover, simple, resilient under the ice, useless wings with long effort. The dusty road wooden beyond the rock, the fence posts are ramshackle, trees on horseback. The clouds' soft camel feet obliterate the man and touch him with earth.

EVERYONE HAS A CLUMSINESS IN THEIR ANSWERS contained in a story somewhere in their family. Their sinister immunity comes from that which has been added to the night, cloudy and still as an exhibition in a church. Among the graves of the first dark shapes drifting in, she was the first woman to be brought there, lying among clothes, when the wreckage flames carried back the bullet to earth, behind the black village church with bearers handing the box to the man who worked in the office. The sky was green above the crowds, but the mother in an instant signalled the end; the memory of the triumphant cheer caught in the light as they swirled over the defiant voice. "We had a lovely view." They remembered the astonished cloud. The shape caught by the slow spring, bent in two and sank out of sight.

AT NIGHT PAST THE WINDSCREEN, the only cat was the size of a house. A piece of paper as sharp as an instrument – everything was a name lost for three hours in the racing cold.

A JOURNEY AS TOUGH AS ART. They travel the road heavy with burgomasters, the painted box ablaze for miles, the buildings images of dominant trees, each trunk white as a cloak; the arrival (of the insect) is enjoyable; the face of the town hidden by rocks.

DRIVING FAST was the big danger, and now it is past. Speed has a meaning of its own; speed lets off gases which are determined genetically, distinguished from the static. Like a fire, there are moral implications, as well as circular and triangular patterns.

THE MOTORBIKE pressures the skyline; the black horse turns green; the girls disintegrate fast; the mobile restless people wear flowered clothes; the young grow slow; women release on their knees; the sociological dog says "Jesus!" while scarlet shapes explode.

THE DEATH in the car on the hill at a spot. There was blood on the road. These two came and were tricked that evening. Both were victims – the two were known, and their knowledge brought them close. The disclosures were true and the answer was yes, and that was all. The car had knowledge of the victims, and there was no case. The car was told and owned, and they drove to the spot on the plain; the crash they planned in the field – it was day. The tap on the window wound down and words were used to persuade the car to go away. The need to leave the field was recognized; the keys loaned to the victims were handed to them. They rattled. The watch said time and did not say what he saw. The days were soaked with rain, but he was a man who did not look at the time. He had the keys, and his wristwatch stopped, with only a few minutes in it.

THE PRISONER DIED AS RESULT OF THE SKILL OF THE CONSTABLE. The Lord Chief Justice "could see nothing incongruous". The widow was no worse off; she would travel first class at no extra charge. Her husband had been killed by the police driving straight at him. Her new car would contain picture windows individually controlled; she would reap tremendous benefits; she would recover damages from the insurers. Yet she rejected proposals yesterday that would cost

£15,000. Despite the apparent absence of the recommendations to be published shortly, this would result in a nil award, because she had failed to complete formalities. Her skill must have been impaired by the amount of alcohol consumed. The error of law was not the result of the law. A second and third car would be examined, and crashed about an area occupied by spectators and other observers.

THE DANGER OF PAVEMENTS. A hundred and eight are known to have died.

NOW GO SILENT, fast, flexible, by train slung from pillars above streets. The rocketing acceleration is limited only by what (passengers) can accept.

THE SULLEN TRAIN CRUMPLES SUICIDALLY. The carriages abound with names, blankets, trousers, falling soot and dusty remnants, hell of old life, tiny smoke-black blankets disinfected by mountains, the necessary stony shore, vertebrae and rusted bottles; their faces have sheep's heads; the wild weather as the rails lengthen; there are no chairs and faded curtains; several million people travel with exposed wires and random glasses levelling off in the whipped wind roaring in the middle of the nowhere wire; poles of tin whirl over the beginning to darken invisible grey geese; the headstones hurl in the drunken sky with no warning; the wife is thrashed in the air for a minute; the graceful foot is pressed to the earth of smoke; the hard ribs crack; you can hear the fires warn each other, and the firewood and skins for thirty seconds died among orange flares. The bride is incapable of swimming; she has changed her eggs in the supermarket for mutton chops, and she travels to her house for basketball. She leaves the rows of scrubbed crosses in the shrinking land; the antirrhinum rustle of sheep who say to each other there is no grass, there is plate glass for two weeks without stopping. Their eyes refuse to lamb in modern purple; the price is 3/6 a pound. Proudly the bride's fingers are ice-green; her prize-winning children will be born there; the other wooden wife buys work in winter; the ancient lady is deep and crinkled; four dogs stand in the lake at night; the horse is thick with blue ice; the house is covered with metal; you see men on the roof blown down from the clouds and grumbling at the hail half a mile wide.

SURVIVORS OF THE VOLCANIC AGE before industrial eruption thrust them, forced them, to fall into the notorious soil. They had the convulsed glass feeling of the coming of steam that destroyed the green mountain. Not only this, but the one who fell thought he was five miles from the floor. His lump of a wife had disappeared; he was left a man of fifty-seven with two sisters, two goats who came to him when they were cold. He faced the difficulty of desolation, the solitary tiny. He saw something new against the hill – its face was glass.

THE GLASS CONSISTS IN GLASS, spaces, six abstract people, several psalms in one character, a screen against which the modern angel grew. Through the window and miles away, for a long time God ran from the frightened face towards his own, at least once and probably more times. (Remember, he came down.) Cathedral colour skills are different from a house: the cathedral contributes fire to keep God alive. In the green field, the common ground, he is alive and well. The glass is divided – stretched across the floor in the form of water – the effect and texture of a town. I come back deeply drawn; the wool in the window holds out the light; a surface can never be flat; strong reflections confuse the problem of light. I must avoid prayer – the mad experience.

"OUR HOUSE IS NICER THAN CHRIST'S." The Cardinal is right. The Pope has to put up with 180 rooms and a series of witty tapestries. The rowdy, cheerful Pope is untouched by his exotic environment; he pours tea; his lady is willowy; the Christian executive has bony knees. His Christmas is as big as Selfridges (he is a Roman Catholic), where he cooked a turkey recently. He spent the war with the Duce* hugging the bust of a beautiful young woman. He never fully recovered from his wartime experiences. What remains is plenty of Holy Roman Empire, and statues which Mussolini used for target practice. His grandfather was hung by the state; now he lives in a hall of mirrors. He is asked to give weddings to the Texas Division of the US Fifth Army, and when he returns from these outings, with the people lined up all day for the ceremony, he puts on his hat, covered with the signatures of the Commonwealth Cricket Club. When they see him coming, the guards vanish down the corridor with loud shrieks, and he says "You can't blame me for that. They accepted my invitation to attend", and it is true – they survive unharmed.

THE SOBER SWISS ARMY LIVES ON FISH – not that it matters.

CARESSING THE IVORY CARVING, THE STONE POPE HAS NOTHING TO DO, only private pleasure. He puts the glass down gently, turns away the image, finds the one he has just left, examines the next with the same technique. Mouthing rubbish, the Pope circles the delicious object, enjoying the amorous proceedings in public.

BEAUTY UPSTAIRS – part of the glamour of private amuse-ment – the sexual enjoyment of angels. The infant Christ is well advertised; the postcard business keeps your eyes open to the theme of legs and reverence; a nun walks through to find the apartments closed at noon.

THE CATHOLIC FAMILY IS PAID BY RESULTS, judged every month by performance: we believe in sixteen million kids getting really fat and big.

EVERY TIME GOD GRINNED THE WOMAN SAID SEX. After one suicide His family made a million. Human is what he was. Jesus is ninety-five per cent the sexual thing. Heaven is an adult relationship, hell a dead loss. Confession is wish-fulfilment. Naked women murder children; a Rolls Royce is an abomination. His face is covered in jewels. "I can sit for hours with a young man of forty-five."

EVERYONE LAUGHS TWENTY-ONE TIMES when the Pope gives something away. "Like hell", when his secretary told him he earned £50,000 a year. Convinced that he should be in an infirmary, his solemn bank manager says the kids adore him. He is ill, he is crazy, he is unique. Whenever he is not feeling well, they talk about success to cheer him up. It's a deal he has with God; a giggle in hospital. When his eleven-year-old boy fell from a tree, nobody said he was not dressed decently; a sweet was placed alongside his head. His hair was dyed or dying, but you could never detect it from watching.

IN THE DANCE HALL HE WAS INVITED TO LAY HIS HANDS ON, full of the sounds of sex and the dangers of money, hungry for youth, for the sixth-former in extraordinary clothes. The concrete cock grew naturally; the priest was mucking about with her tits. "So I asked her to come and see me; to have a talk with me." And a lad passing says, "Why don't you wear a mini?"

WHEN THE BLOND PRIEST bought a flat for his "Mother", the effect was fantastic. The Duchess distinguished herself; she appeared in church in her uniform, carrying a teddy bear and wearing white trousers, shaking her head as he walked by.

IT IS NECESSARY TO DIVERSIFY PEOPLE. Every dolly has a tremendous personality. In their young days they wore trousers. The girl was teating a small boy of ten; he remembers being taken from his mother. It was the horror of war: his home was under guard; he was taken before he could escape quietly. The qualified doctor set fire to the empty building. The patient having a baby wore a large flowered hat. The policeman was called Lilian: "I enjoy a long skirt," he says. "Being pregnant is very primitive."

I WANT TO TALK TO YOU (ABOUT MATHEMATICS). I want to if you like express the impossible. I believe in luck. If luck goes against you, you've made a mistake.

I'M A FAILURE. I have the least reason for surviving. Poverty is part of the punishment. There is little doubt that the Board ensures that my family does not starve. My wife, anyway. My wife and I were children in whose mind the need did not occur. No money, she not being here. Everything seems to come to me for bills. You can assume that the suburban machinery has broken down; the broken plaster lying for months; my poem on the poverty of the land stretching down the length of the room. I don't know, I think I would have gone mad. I have grown used to it now, but when you go out you see faces skipping at you; you know – you know what's in their minds. Besides, I don't know many people in London at this point.

HE THINKS WITH A POINTED BEARD. He is conscious of skill and tone. His friend and rival lives in Wolfe Street, Dundee. His poetry experiment is a verse a day. "I never use 'I' – it is never the right word." When friends arrive, he goes out for a walk around the block.

HE STUDIED THE WORLD WAR IN A LIBRARY. He formed a friendship with war for ten years; he was considered austere and regular; he showed himself geometric, oblique. He was born in Europe – especially Paris; his home was broken and dispersed. In a New York hospital he was invited to kill a man; he said OK; his postcard asked for expenses and a first-class hotel. A gun became part of his life; he lived on the edge of a knock on the door that would come in and start chucking everything around.

MEN IN STOLEN FLYING SUITS: "WE ARE HERE TO KILL, AND WE ARE GOING TO."

SHOOTING IS STILL A DANGER, although the risk is scientifically acceptable. A policeman in London is inclined to disbelieve statistics. In one sense he carried a gun to murder, but he was stopped from making too much of the experience. He was armed; he killed a man accidentally on principle – his first step in the war against crime. "I believe in arming Britain's police," he said. "We cannot simply refuse guns." He saw hundreds of policemen killing a man; the cornered body was armed; some 5,000 pistols were issued, either nervously or fatally (anyone could take a gun into one of the finest schools in the world). The criminal was ill-informed about his death. His ignorance had two aspects: in Brazil they had shot off his legs; they were careless in the use of the pistol.

THE POLICE had come down to the bar to seize the staff of the hotel. Television on a shelf of bottles was a landscape which had not been seen before. The police were accused of kidnapping. No one would talk in the nightclub. The gang two years ago was a menace to society; each man took his gun to a separate town and stayed there for a period of up to five years. The local police had seen the commercial possibilities. They had taken a party of villains for traditional roast pork and a diet of bombs alfresco. The situation of the mountain people was dangerous; they had done something wrong; the donkeys had drunk too much of the fascist landscape. Their deformed lawyers were mentally deficient; their savagery was concentrated in the poorest region. The Marxist politician began to tell his two kidnappers that he had seen his cousin shot for carrying a photograph of Gagarin. The murder of a man a hundred miles away on the steep hillside made the lawyers' fortunes in the summer heat. They made sixty million a year from the heat and dust. When it came to money-making, the island was like nowhere else; for the mountain children there was no change. The top-secret and successful church appeared in essence the same as the old-style bandit. The police seemed indifferent so long as tourists were shot for austere reasons. On August 12th a priest shot his wife, then killed himself, but that confirmed what the communists had been calling him for a decade: a highwayman, an extortionist. And no gun was found.

SHOT DOWN IN GUN-PLAY before he could be brought home to his suburb in June, reconciled to justice, coaxed out of crime before he veered south, he followed the brilliant windfall. He knew the signs of property deals, the profits in killing. Now forty-three, his impatience was apparent; Ky created the brutal occasion with anyone. His capacity for elastic violence outwitted his bodyguards. His property company unearthed large numbers of murdered men, and in the poor light attempted to sell two hundred. Last Wednesday, when the rotting bodies were delivered, the actual state of the poor-quality meat was defined by the English. The language used had been obscure; the legal owner had an imperfect right. The alternative argument noted the antecedent death, and this was taken as a sign of progress. Since they had fallen behind with their payments that morning, the bodies of two men had been disintegrating rapidly. I don't suppose that they were killed by killers.

HUMAN BEHAVIOUR IS ABSOLUTELY JUSTIFIED. You cannot argue with war. The edge of the rope will not keep quiet; the intimidated child will say things to you until silenced by slaps and threats. There is no point in arguing with people – they are too frightened.

HONG KONG IS A CLUTTER OF WAR TOYS. The bodybuilding industrialist wishes to live for a hundred years, as long as his business instincts flourish. He packs his pills in bags; the new-style heated ceiling mats have conquered death. Last year was the year of the low table; fish were guillotined on the low table. He is able to buy beauty; colour magazines are his hobby; daintiness can be recognized in his home by the smell alone. One of the bonuses of the Vietnam War is that he can rent a home for life for 1,000 dollars, and death, for some, means happiness. Six hundred years won't stop that war: business needs fragile peace for a year, then violence every year for ten years. The industrialist says that people who do not rush about are lazy – they can do nothing – they are defeated by a single blow. Though this man avoids the trials of war, he puts four lumps of sugar into his opinions. His enemy resists by doing nothing. "There is a war on." And that is what he needs; everyone defends the war; the landlord must have it; the Government is elected for war; the soldiers give stability. For taking an egg you go to jail – the practice is not modern. The people are too ignorant to own a coal mine, but gangsters do good business – they run the roads and ports; the puppet makes money from the ideal way of life. Do not talk peace with the cruel people; the lips of the big stomach will learn nothing. The word in the room is calm and remote; the war talk screams overhead; the police drink pale tea; justice is expensive everywhere; it filters through the barrier of names. The soldier is called patriot until the sudden sea of fire stops the semi-red street. Petrol pours down the paper-thin man. The bar-girls add to the flames.

"CHEMICAL GESTICULATIONS OF CHAOTIC HUMANITY IN THE VAST AND SHATTERED EAST." The official explanation is back to normal. The flooded river is remembered for seven hours. The sun forgets about human beings, in the cool green coma in the middle of May.

SUNSHINE PAINTS THE SIDE OF THE MOON. The new name dazzles from the bottom of the street. Indisputably British faces blossom in the trading centre; the bourgeoisie is growing at the root. Non-military rifles are sold on the open market; the pale-skinned recipients show a profit; the damp white ladies are diminishing; the attractive Indian is a strategic asset. Things were going on with loose grey discipline everywhere, except on the other side of the street, where the communists carried guns in their trousers. The Chinese years ago knew the smell of rebellion under the floorboards; now the plastic bomb had liberated it. They sniped with guns in the streets; from the gloom of the girlie-bars the net scalps shone scented white, nipples ringed by orange lights, two breast areas each clean stone. Police were riding cars down the corridors between houses; despair in forms was being announced; the smell of the European produced order; the people sprang back out of existence; nihilism made a series of steps past boats of earth; the Government was going to dump the rebels into the sea.

OFFICIAL FRANTIC DISCIPLINE IN A BLUE SHIRT GREETED EVERYONE; the Governor at the bar accompanied the martial music; as he gripped the bottle the tropical shrubbery fell into the ammunition box. After the Governor was killed by broken glass, the Government fixed the price for rooms without windows. When the widow went north to visit the man who owned the best hotel, she was made to swim for it. Beggars from the street dragged through her hair; she saw the dead man loud and grinning and several hundred miles of grease above the royal photograph. When each bottle of water costs six shillings it is not hard to kill a man with a budget spent on keeping lice abounding in his hair.

THE FELLOW WHO IS LOW KEEPS HIS HEAD TO THE GROUND, but the speculator practises self-reliance. He is someone who makes a study of money throughout his life. He trebled his million in ten years. His hands are brighter than we have; the rare millionaire of the dream; the fizz of the boom; disease of the brain. Regardless of the tricky figures, he is totally involved in money more than ever; the solid gold plates are for his pleasure (his customers don't want to lose him). His crocodile boots get bigger; give him a fiver for his gold-plate watch; he has four cars, a song and dance in the office, aeroplanes outside his house. This individual exists as a prototype; he can weigh as much as four. His business is creative work – making something out of nothing. He cannot think or feel without absolute dedication, since the day is his own to feel whatever he likes in the place he has devised as an extension of himself. On his way down the street, on the subject of misleading those who thanked him, the advertising man kept four bottles of good blended sales drive. He took care of his mail and won the friendship of at least one big dealer, a sleight-of-hand middle-rank salesman whose company ultimately suggested the broadest big-stock profits. His personal secretary had been wrapped up in a happy device for altering the rental property, which seemed the coming thing. Blanche went heavy when she had worked out the corporate salary rises formally before she left the office. The conference was over before anyone could gather from his call to his lawyer that his account of his daily expenditure had been underwritten by an insolvent operator. It would be legal, for a few minutes each day, if his plans were successful.

ANYWAY, HE HAD KNOWN TWO QUEENS, both typical of their day, and each in her way was best. He has sympathy for the kids who go out to work, in good weather and in bad. In his small office in Lower Regent Street he is pretty pleased with the way the girls wear their hair long – he likes the way they're shaping.

LIQUID GREEN HAIR IS ABSURD. No, don't.

THE CROTCH EXPERIENCE was different: soft fastenings at the thighs; hold the shoulders; ankles emphasize the impact of schoolgirls in school buses; seeing them makes him quickly fatigued; the single-decker is best – their windows wide, he identified them standing in the aisles; but still, this was manufactured reality – totally new, still in the experimental stage.

LAST YEAR HE WATCHED THE GIRLS ON THOSE MODELLING JOBS – more than a dozen of them in his sights. He laughs at the behaviour of the female. He is somebody who contains few problems; musical talent instils values. His successful childhood is framed above his desk slowly and clearly – he had that much realism; he isn't enjoying his daydreams any more. For ten years the driven male slowly and clearly through each day. The wealthy fanatic exerts pressure – what counts is pressure – but where does the mind wander to?

THE GAME OF OBJECTS, newspaper illogicality, the female attitude towards fun, the accurate instrument indicates blemishes, pursuing the man in his own house.

HE SPENT UP TO FIFTY DOLLARS in a French restaurant with the girl who came for two hours' study, his sports jacket shouldered with vice and corruption as the furred girl explained the geography of Europe. In the capital of the gold city they had fallen in love as they stared out of the windows at the river police.

HE EXPLAINS WHAT SHE SEES, familiar with the words she does not know. His voice prevents her from joining the group. He tries to remember the talking of his children, as they draw the young shape, the brilliant green minute. "I have watched Maureen many times." The painted grin, the serious steps in the room, the voice says, "Dear, it is doubtful whether she will understand."

REGENT STREET HAS A WHALE'S JAW. A small sunset attracts trade; horizontal layers of Dunlopillo keep the place prosperous. When the street is decorated for Christ, fruit is stuck to the windows in the morning.

HE REMEMBERED THAT THE ROMANTIC YOUNG LOVED MONEY; the snowing and the snow go hand in hand; the Victorian bandstand was red and yellow; the long people walked back slowly; the windows would like to see them; they walked through orange snow; the street lights shone on white cardboard; she said she wanted sleighs to appear in the shop window, with floodlights at night. Her kisses were from Europe, and other things were changing – perhaps it was to do with his money.

PRAWN COCKTAIL BLOWN AWAY.

SHE WAS NOT LONG AT THE OFFICE OF POLITE THANKS AND REFUSAL. He drove to her place when something was wrong. They had one beer in his lovely automobile, and soon they were moving around the blocks they had seen before, as he told her carefully of his love and rage. She enjoyed meeting the troubled folding days; she thought progress was like putting on a suit. "I missed you" – and she said other things behind the chauffeur's back. "I will take you, since you remind me. I want to talk to you after dinner." He swallowed before he drove to where she wanted, with difficulty. She felt at home in the Mercedes. He thought she said she had fixed a time, and decided on coming to his flat. Since dinner this had happened several times. Perhaps she was going to murder him in his office: he was going downhill emotionally. He received a message after watching the Mercedes take her back to the café where she had gone for more time. The quick horn handle at the side; the Mercedes was pregnant; the pedals covered with flesh; the bucket seat looked chic; the coloured beautiful automobile drove narrow like a dirty knife. The motor sound was faint; it would go better, thank you. It was necessary to be some distance away; her expression was too much; the worry would prevent him from thinking; he talked of whatever it was he feared from the conversation. He was silent until after he was sure of the road, bringing the flowers and lighting her cigarette, saying nothing to the car door. The effort of keeping his voice low helped contain the tones of the well-shaped head of the girl sitting beside him. The pressure from the corner of her mouth made her nag the bucket seat. Women were graceful branches spreading over us to protect the sun from the wash from our mad shock.

IT'S HARD TO FORNICATE IN YOUR OWN HOME – IT'S BETTER IN THE PARK. One of the reasons is the horror of women indoors. The girlfriend of the reserved Englishman has waited until today, when men and women are kissing in her back garden. The roadside picnic is the strangest revival since Chinese became fashionable. The dull and careful park-keeper has a job on the public payroll, and his determined alcoholism is unquestionably moral. The majority of park-keepers have a certain lightness of spirit: he will assume the old-fashioned homosexual to be buying flowers. But sex and drink in a public place is a vice.

A SMALL, QUIET SQUARE, YOU UNDERSTAND – a shop on the edge of a joke. Step out of the sun into a drink. Inside the flat, there was half a melon, a jumble of fascinating coffee spoons, four doors painted scarlet, a refrigerator cut in half, yesterday's pile of pussy's pieces, a cat in the middle of the refrigerator without moving its feet. He turned the dovelike fish whose voice was higher on both sides; the blood flowed over; he kept the blood inside the bowl, then took off his coat.

THE COATS ON THE BED ARE BUSY TALKING. Girls of eighteen must be married in a dream in a mangled room. She was warm with doubt and shy in areas of life. The gloomy morning blossomed; he knew everything, every her and what they were; her lovely skin gave him enormous energy. They had a discussion for hours that winter – the most beautiful naked-body sensation – able to bath together and get married. It was one of those middle-class things.

THE TWO TOOK THEIR WORDS TOGETHER BY THE USE OF LIPS; he cut the words out of her nose; he would prefer her teeth. Her heart was a sound in his opinion, with infinite possibilities; her moving parts worked well. The police were involved in the business; they arrived at his office to discuss the extortion case; she knew nothing; her eye was ruled inadmissible. The trial for rape was the same. The allegation was withdrawn before the offence was committed.

BAD WEATHER is the opportunity to opt out of Saturday nights, and for newly-weds this encourages saving. The heating bill is high, the snowball escapes from the rosy houses, the instructions to the thermostat are hazily defined. The girl in the green bath looks ridiculous, glaring up and turning round, asking who made her wear her clothes in the bath, thinking there was no reason – at least, so it seemed to me.

WHAT HAPPENS USUALLY WHEN YOU MEET? Special display in the gardens; the glamour of contemporary art. Meeting is a reproductive process, behind a row of misty bicycles, where the observation of death grows older, and women are easily available.

RUMOUR ran and never stopped along the corridors of the tennis clubs; youth hatching plans under lamp-posts to catch the eye of female cars with noisy open doors. The art schools made plots to run away and hide with flimsy girls swooning on number plates. They were friends of such wild occasions, discussing the history of civilization and ideas. He decided neither to leave her now nor to support her nightly at 9.25 p.m. in his soldierly arms in an orange daze of whisky drunk warm in the brewery.

THE GIRL IS A PURPLE DRUG substantiated by fact – the same social escape as drink. Parents, on the other hand, make no difference, especially when they are married. The fascinating child will wish to marry her father; she will avoid an abortion. Many girls wish to marry their own child; interestingly, many girls pass through this stage. The tendency is towards the ideal. Progressive girls take care of the figure and tend to live as if they were pregnant. Some of them wish to marry their father; some of them never tell the truth; freedom prevails; the pattern is provoking.

A SINGLE MAGAZINE IN AMERICA SOLD 30,000 COPIES LAST YEAR: write and tell them why their pretty pictures and all those dreary things reflect the times. The first pornographic thing all over made £300; the imported American production is enjoyed in cinemas in Ireland; the coffee bar delights in it. Already Warsaw is famous for racy drawings and subtle catching literature. The connoisseurs of the developed bust between boots helped to shape the appetite for everything, for heavy leather, anything; delighted with globes, the actual balls are mostly vulgar; the bit of sex is unintentional. I've had a very visual wife for years – my wife Margaret had the formula right, always picking the size that sells, encouraged by her coloured personality.

THE ULTIMATE CAN BE VERY DREARY; the law recognizes the likely lass; most get prosecuted after all. Eighteen female persons are in the area of police operations; they don't have to walk through the common gateway any more; they don't have to fight each other with fists. The lawyer in the courtyard is well heated; he visited the women in their living quarters; the restaurant is as hygienic as possible. The good-health girls also exist, though on a cold day they are not permitted beyond the glass barrier. The young blonde girls are very desirable; they sell milk; the men are not allowed to drink while they lie in the girls' wombs, though they're very keen on coffee. The middle-aged wallpaper, fawn furniture; the walls are sadder than before; the cuddly blouses are divided between nine. 500,000 women are too cold; for five days they happen naturally; that's nice, but they expect a profit as well.

SEX AND VICE IS THE COUNTRY'S BIGGEST INDUSTRY. Most towns have some local area where they keep their little girls. Luckily for their fathers most things happen where lots of allegedly sexy sights are concentrated: they know where they stand. The famous street, the mystery of oho; no one knows much or cares less; the streets are full of theatres. The street is a street that smells of sex. The dead food is all hamburgers. Natural people's minds are caught by wicked sausages. The automatic crook is a food machine. Dodgy doormen look like single women; the square pavements say what they would say. A very clean dwarf took my shoulder and gave me welcome in the afternoon. It's bound to happen decently. The girls have huge neon signs till they are pulled down. Sex maniacs are fascinating to experts; their scattered illusions are differences that separate the breasts. The gentlemen arrive from the Oxford college, but the nights are designed by gangs; successful lads reach everything new; the stained hand breaks bricks; their fists go round the block; they invest their money in women.

THE CENSORSHIP BOARD HAS FIVE HEAVY BREASTS, but bouncy noise is not its way to happiness. Sex is pain in a brown paper bag, a product of very thin people. The Scottish cuntry expects nothing better than sex by manipulation, and this is permissible, particularly in public life. The over-eager student is banned officially or unofficially; the passionate dissimilarity of boys and girls is attacked by the right-wing MP. The unfree member at nine o'clock on Saturday makes money enthusiastically; he gets up and leaves the room; he desires life in ignorance; he wants something which sells in a shop. The business of sex is understandable; it is unpleasant; the joyless depend on the local brothel and not much else. The talentless politician is not going home; his personal history is disheartening; his hero is a fish; he has regrets; he misses the pop influences; he needs his dream of glory. He thinks the boys will get tired if a book is banned for nine years. The influential persuader says no, and authority in a black cap says don't marry a nun who has been pepped up. Thirty-seven per cent of the people are curious about sex in a churchyard and smile at the thought. The mind is clean till it gets its hooks on a book.

THE LOCAL MAGISTRATES were misfits, eccentrics, boozers, who would say anything for money, with a function not unlike the man who does not get worried when he takes over a haunted house.

CYRIL CANNOT BE ALONE. Best with someone – old or young. It doesn't matter which. No opinion is comforting: too sophisticated or too simple. Even for admirals the sky grows darker, and he had discovered that for vicars, headmasters and others the sea rises higher. The prudent institutions remain alone like saddened women. During the years he had felt dispossessed, without allies, not in the right place. He had written articles seeking to help materially, or dealing with matters spiritual, but everything had been said in the universities, and the various churches were unhelpful. They all believed in the erosion of property, while he was growing richer. The infernal unions produced astonishing struggles every year. These people were neither patriotic nor honourable, and they became more dangerous in the summer.

THEY ACTUALLY PASSED A LAW SAYING THAT UNION JACKS MUST BE WORN IN THE HAIR, and all girls must be inspected or thrown in the lake. The pretty girl drinking with the millionaire refused, and was most emphatic, her red hair done up in magnificent black. For three days repeated excuses had been provided, as they danced to the river-pattern riffle in the garden. The politician's wife had her hair multicoloured in the morning; the magistrates were dancing easily, the stuffed skirt waiting for them under the oily talk about culture, the moist pressure of flesh behind the bar, the official sound waves mixing with the gurgling music, the drunk flow of music with young ladies swung upon the water throng. The lovely girl turned red and white with fury; the beautiful main street swept towards the lake, down the avenue of hills on either side of the flags of the progressive nations. While the Indians submit to the whip, the Queen in diamonds looks like a god; the fizzy orange has a fine head. The mother country shall be in the headlines drinking beer; the banana war (Britain's unique contribution to the history of stink) – the banana war is what you've got to do.

THE CUSTOM OF AFRICA has since been written: Can we eat boiled sticks? He walked a few feet, then whispered: "Four tins full of flour, please." The motorized flour weighed less than forty-five pounds.

READY TO HURL YOURSELF INTO AFRICA? You may end in your neighbour's lap with four large dollops of droppings of elephant. The black cook misread the sinister clause, and burnt down the house without noise; there was no sound from the branches being moved across the room, only the groaning from the child in the high cot. Night is impossible; you gaze at it, weaponless. From the window of your vehicle, wait the night (no movement going round in circles); a rare, black, swift African dawn came down, boring in Kodachrome. In ran fifty elephants; a battered tree stuck in the mud; pedestrians with inflamed faces stared rudely at the ladies' legs. The black-headed chauffeur made fruity sounds, spicing the sandwiches the most expensive way. The choice is yours. Bodily intimacy in the morning; the first exposure of the child's cock; the animal noise was terrible; thousands of addresses mumbling in the atmosphere. They fell together in the six-foot hole; a hundred yards of whispering windows open to the rain; exhaustion loaded onto black handlebars.

THE STREETS NAME THEMSELVES AFTER LAVATORIES; the discipline of classes is always in use; to maintain the power of the bottle-drinking Queen.

NOW WAS THE OPPORTUNITY FOR INTELLECTUALS TO SALVAGE THE IDEA OF THE HONEYMOON AT WINDSOR TO INCREASE THE PRESTIGE OF THE QUEEN. Limelight gets results; American confidence assures support; the frigid Queen is managed with dynamism and skill, but it is doubtful if her compatible partner will keep his mouth open without talking too much. The enigmatic grin is more aggressive than arrogance, and the immediate issue has become the equality of manual workers with peeresses in their own right. Now waiters will expect similar treatment; the Government is so feeble. Morality is about money, anyway; the Church collects its income tax, and the transition from the absurd low-grade civil servant to those who rule the land is unpredictable. The mechanical eye of the chairman of the board sorts figures and writing; official contraception is bought cheaply; the country seems sinful; the police are sold at 100-per-cent profit; men found impersonating royalty are sent to Scotland; raspberries wear an expression of natural nobility; the unmarried girl waits outside the liquor store penetrating the marked man with gleams of sunshine.

IN THIS CHAOS THE SCOTTISH PRINCESS WAS COVERED CARELESSLY WITH YELLOWING MEDALS. Twenty minutes later she murmured from the window sill because she was so pretty, "I should have shaved there" (pointing) "like the French girls do; then you would have loved me in the garden." She said she was never fresh enough, though she ground her teeth herself; it was so easy. "Like other girls I wear short skirts; I am light and fluffy like the English." She was not against old photos, souvenirs and maps, but she liked to meet new people.

OF COURSE WE ALL KNOW HER INTIMATE OPERATIONS.

SHE BORROWED PERFUME FROM THE BISHOP'S YOUNGER DAUGHTER; she had wanted to enter the Church countless times. In Liverpool she had switched to theology; it was frightfully interesting to hit the headlines: the huge amethyst on her hips; her gloves were of particular interest; living in a council house; dressed in a purple cassock – reporters all over the place.

WITH CONTEMPT FOR DARING NAKEDNESS (modern children were undressing too quickly) she said amusing things. She did it perfectly. Playing the adult beautiful, she behaved like a pound of bacon.

HER NEWEST MINISKIRT HAD A MOUSTACHE FOR THREE WEEKS. Then her stomach began to woman, rejoicing in the sense of permanence. On weekends she worked for charity, and every Saturday night she stayed in bed and opened the big ones. She made a lot of money because she looked honest. "I may sell my mother – we shall see."

WITH THE ACCENT ON DIFFERENCE, the long, low, solidly built sturdy original fabric was the choice of a lady. Timber structure, brilliant white; front door facing pretty against the trees. Like Mrs Murphy she is not interested in the fifteenth century. She said it in the village near the church – a neat clean woman reading potatoes. What is death? Two signs pointing down a hill that isn't there. She stared at water the colour of opal. Beyond the gate was a wonderful wood. Her private glimpse of modern furniture and film in colour hour by hour; the same was true of all the other houses; the curtains fell in peace in nearly every case, with only a pattern in sand remaining. Towering weeds strayed across picturesque beds of air; at breakfast-time a man knocked; all he wanted was sixteen pence a day. The decision was wearing her nightdress;

the mistress was glad to offer four thousand pounds. A man offered sacrifices, living in the open; the lodger living in the third bedroom stepped over the frontier, and everyone smiled; the white bird moved off with part of the fireplace; there were no sounds in the hall. And only one addition had been made to the magnificent sands.

JELLIED EGGS AND CREEPER-COVERED BEANS – the garden was her bed, the lawns a bath of fire. The flute was one of her hobbies; the wooden stave closed over the glass door leading to the sea. The August dress looked marvellous; it was time to change behind the lawn; seven people had a bath; the lady's tie was gay; a lot of people had lived in that street, but now it was nasty down there. Her grandmother died, smothered in ivy. The great romance of her life was an artist who worked a petrol pump. The lonely man had never married.

THE COUNTESS DID NOT MEET HER FAMILY. How would you like to have her superiority?

THE FIRST PAPER MEMORY IS SOMETHING LIKE A HOUSE. My father's father wore a paper hat, but was more interested in plates and cutlery. He went off to live in America, because the ideas of the eighteenth century irritated him.

BALLOONS ARE BLOWN-UP ROMANCES – the frantic dance floor of a wartime film, the northern girl in a trouser suit, the customers in little paper hats.

NOBODY KNOWS HIS OWN FATHER; HE FINDS HIM LOST IN A BAG: he looks sad; he wanted respect for values; he begins his work for civilization on Friday night, depressed by the ignorance of the *News of the World*.

HIS HABIT was to go to a place for years to have his own reactions. He did not want to be told; he wanted to know. The primitive eccentric has lost his memory, his strength to find huge ships on a piece of paper; he looks for his feelings and finds a horse; the river may take years to isolate the ocean.

THE RIVER FLEW PAST THE FUNNEL FROM TIME TO TIME.

RIVERS OF BRICK, curved red patterns dive and fall north and west, lining the roofs with weeds. The walls climb into petals of change and stress; the sign of the road crosses the various bloods and different risings of ancient people. The path is paved with years. Bright hunters shelter in the green valley and the home is painted with purpose. Unnatural wealth is a green fog; the heart seems interior; cathedrals on cliffs like brave omelettes blast the town to bits. The road falls on the town; the church of glass collapses; the unity of time and lime destroys the lives of kings. The driving lights are lit by Ulysses; the gardens shine for miles, splashing white peach.

IT IS THE LARGE CITY. It lies in the middle, at an average height above the sea, between the coast and hills, bounded by plateaux; between the two lies a valley. The river has its source; it flows through lakes. It is so large. The highest point is an artificial hill. Subject to changes in temperature and differences in rainfall from year to year, forests occupy the area; it has trees. The surface was shaped by ice; retreating water carved valleys – valleys connected by gullies, split by the blanket of lakes. It occupies the land. The marsh is now a garden. There are few hills. From the rubble of hills, remnants of woods, the nucleus; the absorbing and transforming expansion, the rulers advanced the boundaries to the sea. Lines of streets connect the gates. The wide circle is now complete. The metropolis is built. The factories form towns. Sewage spoils the lakes. The exit road is the favourite part of the city. The office of mayor forms the centre of the zoo. The famous court and prison afford lovely views over the airfield; intercourse is not allowed, though permits are issued for limited periods.

MILLIONS LICK THEIR WIVES. The death houses are bricked up. Police protect their lives. Energetic foreigners increase trade; the quick-witted work in the central market. The city is force; the Minister of Order determines policy with the concurrence of representatives. The constitution is operative. All meet the Government for consultation. The city cannot feed itself. Cows are edible. An abattoir was set up. Water is purchased by the municipality from wells within the area. Electricity is supplied; the modern power is fired with dust. Horses are abolished. There are private cars. Trains go in and out. The underground is low, owing to the low ground.

THE LEAF AT HIGH ALTITUDE withers before the cold; the less delicate stay soft and pliable. The grey spout rises; the forkful of snow is thickened with beer; the systematic cruelty of cold increases. As the ice-like mountain forces the shiver of weakness, the sun-silk hair uncurls its beautiful colours; the menthol-fresh actress in her spring flush spurns the unlit set; the hair on the young buds brings unhappy memories of milk; for six minutes she seems less strong; she looks for milk in her memories; her delicate years are used; the years ago are prized; the lemony feeling is warm and long.

MONLANGUOROUS, VERY. The hair falls apart, and the amused actress exploits herself eating fishes. Now I do not know what else to photograph. She hopes her knees go click each time. Her fierce look shows her juicy inside. (She keeps her honey in a sponge bag for a time.) Massage of the bottom might be necessary, if you can reach – probably in the morning, certainly at night.

THE DIRECTOR sat down on a chair on a mountain; the numerous megaphones shouted: "He is not here." The palaces were tipped upside down when civilization appeared, some of the buildings were in pandemonium; the white-stone stairways would not reach up; hundreds of new brick homes appeared; ten fortresses were locked and guarded by well-paid men; the experts said the city built by men was now in ruins; the extras who lived on the other side had to knock to gain admission.

TWO SWISS CAMERAMEN, WITH PANGS THAT ENDURED, PREOCCUPIED WITH THE FICTITIOUS IMPOSSIBILITY OF PURCHASING REALITY, TOOK PICTURES OF THE MORNING SWIFTLY. The character of God they were substituting for money – the money involved in God; the idea was for Him to be driven by car, and someone had to change the wheels, provide the tyres. God was in his late forties, short, dapper and very likeable. Sure they paid, more than for anyone except the Queen. "Just look what's at stake. We can't afford any cuts, or the sound will not be heard." They shared His belief in His mass-pulling power, His insistence on starring in the power-movie. But there would be mistakes in rainy weather; they must wait for sunshine; spending dollars entertaining the actors overnight. Or He might get killed in one hundred and ten explosions, each equivalent to disaster. The money must still be found, both for union recognition and for insuring His face against damage to His business. "If you're interested in nuts, we're trying to avoid the possibility of disaster. We're in a competitive situation and people have an idea one way, sexing up the scenes, mixing up the races, going too fast and claiming to play the game with the story of what is happening. Every year somebody does, somebody risks, he will be 'more authentic'. But we're not worried when somebody else gets vicious currently at fake speed." They were shooting the world in the insanity of it, contracting to re-equip the superstructure whatever they felt. They were careful to remain boring; nothing compared with the tedium of the plain. Their confidence was gone. "But we can make everything: Names, owners, machines. Everything we've got is good as gold."

THE TRUE GOLD IS GOLD EACH YEAR; it is a simulated black-gold market supplied by the scales of London. Zurich weighs three quarters of a handful of coins; non-communist Vienna has a couple of bars tucked away. What will happen when the demand for coins is confined to the chap who mends the road? The market is secret, the gold itself is kept in kilo bars. I know lots of people over the Pyrenees worth £800,000 an ounce. The banker suggested £3 an ounce. Most afternoons tons of gold vanish into the cellar; the son of a wealthy soap alone spent £167 million in Spain, with plenty of money left in fibre boxes. The Greek remembers the armoured train: "My daddy said to buy it." How great the desire for the globe. Bargaining the family, changing their money; others in Europe also see gold inside the vaults. We have less money and less death. We have seen the electrically operated door, sovereigns hidden in Eastern Europe; it is possible to buy gold with gold. People are forced into gold. If a man dies with gold in his pockets, his son quickly removes the coins.

THE MONEY HIDDEN IN SWITZERLAND was left there by Germans, who had turned the landscape into lead.

THE GREY ROCK FLUTTERED ACROSS COUNTRY; the pine trees suited the occasion; thousands of extras evoked joy; the skylines of clichés were ugly with church spires; the calm identity of love secreted in glaciers.

GREY SUITS, ALL CONFIDENT COPIES OF PARIS, THE CITY OF PLEASURE, unfolded in the morning as policemen shut the gates on teenage wings. While Byzantine spectators cheered, the statue from the shaded park was taken to its place on the shores of the lake.

THE FILM SYNDICATE is synchronized and linked; their costs are up one per cent; disaster is happening all the time; £10,000 is regularly lost. Elderly men in hot nightclothes paint Bardot in neon; her breasts are remodelled in concrete. "We never stop trying to have the stars knocked about. I expect we will end by having them torn to pieces."

SWING IN. With a zoom lens blot out everything above; the level of energy and time from all angles focuses in your hand one evening. You can point personally. The specialized space gives you a child's room. Work on a big scale. A lot of activities become possible. You can show detail in a way that precipitates a revolution. Then, every year for five years, tackle big schemes, use progressive methods. Three cameras encourage imagination; detail sustains interest; choose your subject: the death of Kennedy; the cheap hero. Fill the space on the white wall; discover you can do what television cannot do. Like Cassius Clay, the drawn, torn philosopher, you are too big for the windowless screen. After all, all you need is a girl in a van on the verge of stripping her cotton dress and the mastery of new techniques and technical mysteries.

MARLON BRANDO WATCHED HAMLET, laughed at a phrase in it, held the world in a drink, ran from the office in tears.

EVERY MOOD RECEIVES A FEE. He is an experienced actor whose identity is submerged. Burdened with his bags, his secretary's function is to carry his equipment. There were perhaps a dozen bags, and these enormous weights had to be out by eight o'clock, borne by the slightly built girl in dark blue, who was thus burdened with full responsibility. The film star walked straight out of the hotel and onto the set. She slammed the bags down. All that day he looked like a wrestler, he held out his hand to the taxi-driver, grabbed him by the ear and thrust his head down a hole.

THE OBSOLETE ACTOR WAS IN FACT A DUKE BORN IN GREECE.

THE WOMAN SECRETARY SAID THE DUKE WOULD GO TO BED ANYWHERE, TOGETHER WITH FORMAL PRAYERS. He would do it in the car, anywhere – in the face if she didn't – for an hour and a half on television, with a bottle of sherry and three empties. She married after three years. Then this was something her husband and the Duke took turns at. He spent a week with his wife this summer.

HE WAS ALWAYS IN THE NEWS. And you've got to know that it is not unusual for a familiar face to look this year like an arthritic ready with the right answer. The Duke's your man. When you talk to him he disappears for a month or two, thrusting his hand back into your pocket. His advice inspires you to shut up. He returns smiling with the news that has already been announced. Well above the usual tone, he has been around the world in general. The usual offence for men of this class is failing the tradition of a good family (a load of rubbish in the circumstances). Why should he waste his time and money on those who serve?

HE CARRIES AN ASSORTMENT OF COMPLEX EQUIPMENT AS A FORM OF SECURITY. His tape recorder felt slightly depressed; the wire crawled over the wall. A piece of masonry formed a secret sign. The occurrence in the taxi held religious meaning.

CONVINCED THAT THE WORLD SHOULD LOVE HIS HUGE FAMILY, he needs the help of women to be poetic. He has eight children by friendly women. The star was free on the Riviera, away from amorous adventure for eight years, reading *Time* magazine till dawn, hearing the other sounds of the twentieth-century thing. It is hard to believe the town suit can still create such sounds. The fix resolves the contradictions. To meet his yellow public he comes to London; his stomach is lifted out and broken; his body distresses him. His tall hands thank the man, talking of brothers and thanks.

NOW HE CAN EAT HIS THREE BANANAS. He helped himself at one o'clock in the morning, his mouth of fruit foaming over himself. He forgets his name; he fools the new life in him; his chin holds up the world; the fatigue in his eye crosses the other eye. The world follows the primeval order. He preserves fear of himself at four, but there he is between the living thing and the sea. Until he is dead his family lives too. An aeroplane waits in front of his hotel. The guestbook makes an O till his silver money is found. The American crackles in chapel; destiny can read and write. He will kill the famous chef; his arms gone, he has kennels full of bananas; he encourages photographers; it was he who felt overwhelming in New York.

HE HAS ALWAYS ENJOYED THE TEXTURE OF A HAPPY MARRIAGE, complete with grotesque cripples (the reason why he is labelled master), avoiding the large inhuman ground with tilted shadows.

THERE WERE ELECTRONIC CLICKS OF LANGUAGE as he talked to his wife. The operator had charm. The conversation had a Spanish hand over his face. "Okay," but he was suddenly different. She knew who he was. "Yeah, it's me." It was clear he had been betrayed. It was all right. It was unimportant. He had received and not answered a letter. The lousy dinner encouraged him to stay in New York. The continual rain worried him. He knew he was not there with her good wishes. He got through Paris successfully; the passenger gangway smelled of kerosene. "I told you about my trouble. The painful thing was cured. When I passed through I felt free." He remembered years ago when he slept with his Washington wife in different positions. She liked to cook, but now his wife was five and a half feet tall with sandy-brown husband and respectability. She had been wearing a white linen suit; it had been announced that she would be wearing white. Her relatives had trouble in selecting the guests and telling them to shake hands. In the double room he had a couple of drinks with Anne Marie, and said in passing, "I appreciate those rags." The glass contained comfort enough, but not enough. It was a hell of a life with no roots. They told me to keep going on as before. "Yeah," I said. In 1957 I found something: the advantage of staying in hell. But a permanent girl asks lots of questions. We were running around most of the time; then we moved back to Paris. I found it best to get her out of the way first. I remember her cheerful questions. The answers wouldn't come. Then she stopped writing, and the lawyers were saying... "For Christ's sake!" She stayed some time before she went away.

IT WAS THEN HE PRODUCED HIS PLAN TO SPEED UP LIFE: there were only three terms of life and "It seems to me that we are a hybrid race able to increase speed for ever." He laughed out loud at the remarkable thought.

HIS SISTER THEODORA WAS MARRIED THE NIGHT BEFORE in his castle lined with armour. The groom carried a bouquet of bread in his buttonhole. They had four daughters and a son the next day.

A COUPLE OF LEGS WERE STUCK IN THE WAISTBAND OF HIS TROUSERS. In the village below, he swallowed a bowl of soup and chocolate mascara. His voice was ricocheting thirty miles from Salisbury when his wife flopped in the snow. His capable hands one at a time were eating bread and cheese, carrying on the noisy war in Welsh, with shaved head and fur boots.

NOW HE EXPECTED TO SEE THE KILTED PIPE BAND OF THE SCOTS GUARDS marching and cheering over the mountains and being shot through their old battlegrounds. He cabled the casting director with controversies all the time; he learnt that the Guards were not tall enough to shift the tons of sand against the wall; he was asked to help, but he was tired. He placed his boots on the table, switched the direction of his bulk on the bed, stripped off his military shirt.

HE STAYED IN HIS YACHT FOR 250 DAYS, fastening his teeth onto a paper cup ravenously. He landed south of Nice, then tripped over a giant tree.

THE SHALLOW SEA OF GREY SMILING MATERIAL prolonged the day; he carried the night in his overnight bag. The young woman on the telephone promised the fully equipped recreation he demanded. Next day the well-built delegate from Britain, wearing pearls in his hair – a devotee of silver – made plain his deep respect for private aircraft. Peter Sellers certainly seemed funny trying on his trousers. The lounge filled up with Germans aware of her Swedish shape at the dead end of the long hotel, pursuing her legs between the sheets from spiritual motive. Her bosom grew bigger and bigger until she stopped breathing altogether. "In South America the young women last two months. Here it is possible to strike lucky with loads of francs and make the girl last longer." David Frost laughed joyfully in the great hotel, his little joke a forlorn attempt to create nothing whatever. He had totally subdued his daisy. Frank Sinatra stated his preferences too. The courageous younger sister distrusted him. For three days she lived on cups of tea alone. Christ, he was a Greek sculpture, and like Jesus he smoked hash on and off. Apart from getting high on sacramental wine, he had no personality problems; he had a dynamic wish to play a leading role in public affairs. David Frost was bloody rude to a blonde actress a few minutes before; he finished with a terrified smile; he'd been playing poker with Yvette Mimieux and Gypsy Rose Lee by mistake. He said goodbye to Ted Hill, who loved good conversation.

THE TOUCH OF INSANITY MULTIPLIED HIS FAN MAIL FIFTY TIMES; his incoherence puts him among the biggest. For a year he did his weekly show of gibberish, which it is – it is all beyond reason, putting on the mindspin, the open secret signs of the bigswing each Saturday. Younger Europe is big enough to force him towards the idol industry, getting ready for last year's anarchy. A million dollars develops Messiah, though his supporters claim none of this is relevant; frequent hysterics build his talent with speed, throwing out business like maniacs; the wilder blurs are loved; the blowing howling conflict business with the psychedelic motorbike, and that's where the audience met him on Saturday night – sexily monstrous, obviously there. "I choose pop; I wind to fit the mood." He began to sort through thirteen girls, plastered with lunch and placards. He was a landslide for hours on end, stretched out all over with the long-wave slogan, promising to bring back commercial things like reversible eek radio and immediately win eek or the new girl's climax. "Then I'll be all right and conscientious in all this and wrap things up the way I want with hardly anything for hours on end. When I have Europe I'll spread for hours. I came out alive and worldwide in the end. I'm going again, like I did this afternoon. What's the point? Money's the blahblah maximum point." He has direction;

his assistant Sam has a million dollars in the bank, and his personal photographer has quit, and the rest of his engineers and secretaries plus assorted life-educating flesh shrieked amazingly. The rich and successful man in his chair sweated like he had a sergeant major on top of him. "All this is mine" – neurotically on the floor. His cars were a good show; his career had flair; he made himself. When he came on the air he sends out the sense of man was mad; the producer got out of the way; he started right on his night; the mad show eleven till two – the same wave as the afternoon, all hard-work length; he had a fast dinner, but tonight puts on an average fifteen hours, sorting the swingkids, preparing his pile in fleets of cars, the full fanclaim producing jungles that careered his special trade right across town to eat 500 separate cassettes; the restaurant in his mouth with marvellous food, and this, when he began to suck it, all of this became really expensive; he went berserk with his head for the first time, swinging the waitress on her back, flirting with spirit, insulting himself; she brought him bowls of plums; there was a fight as hard as ever; he was burning time with endless morning music – fifty girls in twenty hours – maniacal by now; a dozen wires and tubes in corners; three more hours hanging on, he pissed on his photographer, giggling in a corner; he stripped most of his girls to the waist; his knees screamed; he howls his eyes open for the eye-opening ultimate climax putting in

THIS MAN WITH CRIMINAL TENDENCIES became mentally ill. He was aware of the colours of his friends. He swiftly attained his object. His stability increased. His own feet were a pleasurable lump of mankind.

HE TELEPHONED HIS LONG-DISTANCE WIFE. "Independent means we're able to lead independent lives. In a bright-green bed we go our own ways. Without a sound it's good for us to play quietly."

AFTER THEIR EVENING TALK, his superior mind slides towards the wordless night. He listens occasionally; her admiration looks at him; he breathes faster; she has moved the dead; her mouth has said nothing.

OUR LINE IS DEAD. A night telephone can cost twelve pounds. Exactly. Yes. Can't do a thing about it. Check each girl in town. Literally impossible. You try to check all those in one night. Can't be done. Inadequate machinery. Going now.

HE RODE TO HOUNDS IN THE MORNING. His three gardeners were loaded with arms and ammunition.

THE DAYDREAM DISCOTHEQUE remained in need of the professional lavender shirt; picture the noise – adolescent Annabel with shock smile exercises on the staircase between songs of intimate toiletry on recording tape. Halfway men with two women coiled around the jockey seat permitted the mother of twins to stumble through the door every four weeks. He replaced his head on the rack, a bit shaky, silky personality sprouting hellos on the home service. He had forgotten the whisky – the melancholy smooth – as silence sinks in the toothless mouth.

LOOKING AT A TELEPHONE means that a woman is an individualist as long as her face works. Her history is another matter that should be opened and written down. The paradox of her reason leads to division of labour; the law and nature of language is involved; the collaboration of telephone and man.

HIS LIBIDINOUS EXPLANATIONS KISSED HER NECK and said: "I'm having a haircut now in Las Vegas tonight." She was often unconscious until quite late at night; she continued to evolve rather than revolt; she possessed mixtures of pain in her bedroom; the badge of the wife of a torturer. Aware of his envy of her hair, she learnt the correct way to decorate her transvestite uniform to cultivate the state of not give a damn.

I'LL LEAVE HIM AT THE RIGHT TIME.

SHE PRACTISES HER LITTLE BIT OF ANGER. But her family responsibilities are indestructible.

THE NEXT DAY HE WAS INJURED IN A PLANE CRASH. His intellect and sensitivity explored those regions after midnight; the practical man, his tie was off – he was killed in action with the physical courage of one strong hand and other disasters. The dirty work is done with sophistication, the silent cufflinks charged with electricity – there's no mistaking the coloured shirt in the flames. The copy of *Look* was a poem. The U-shaped body was getting very mean.

THE WATERS SWIRLED BEFORE HE DIED WITH A KNIFE; the police recorded he was not dead. For twenty-five years his wife had time to gasp; the breakfast on the table turned tragic.

HER FLAT IS A USELESS TEXTBOOK, TWENTY YEARS OLD.

THE FACES AND ATMOSPHERES OF WOMEN LIKE ACTRESSES.

THE FUNERAL CHAPEL FROWNS ON THE DOG LEFT AT HOME. To protect old ladies from the past, the future is picked out on a die.

DEMOLITION BEGAN AT THE CENTRE OF AN ILLUSION: women in a vision of cloaks and coaches; hotels release their men with the last lights of the night; mincing photographer; noisy princess; two canes walking. Thirty street corners were pulled down; the anxious earl overlooking the clattering park as the town houses toppled too. The duchess wanted to speak; the unfashionable people had assassinated the eighteenth century; those who survived danced in offices. The world war was a party in fancy dress. The accidental and esoteric fell like unrecognized bombs at the death of the famous café. The magnetic prostitutes clustered for protection, the gold dresses up and down. They were six in a circular garden, behind the disorderly street of ritzy flats; their house remained a private dwelling.

SKI TROUSERS BREATHED PALE VIOLET. The incredible Jewish room became so hot. The child was swung in the air soon after dinner began. The cook is dressed in black silk; she loves jewels; she doesn't care for the food; her gown would not match the goulash.

THE BROKEN HOME TURNS BROWN. The bottle of love is lost. Lust is brought indoors, to the horror of women whose desires are released in private. They continue to dress in downcast dress, in strained and sober costume. Women in velvet uniform (grey actors) avoid striped poets and fluorescent shock. They miss the adventurous festoons of last summer.

HER BODY BURST AT LONDON UNIVERSITY – an instrument changed her. Without hair or clothes, she moved house; she threw stones at her sister Kath. There was no reason for the groups she had begun attending; the drinking session is reserved for barbarous women; her husband forgot the astral plane. She picked up a living in Ealing, and afterwards in Brighton. The glorious welfare worker could not be drunk, technically.

THE PROBLEM IS THERE ARE NOT ENOUGH FLATS ALLOWED TO EXIST. It is homes. And we all know there have been explosions in families condemned by the Government. There are tremendous bangs on council estates when a flat gets given to a family. The trouble starts when race relations reveal themselves. After all, the pink will continue to exist in family swellings. The families wait for a flat contrary to humanitarianism. The lower classes are rivals at the moment in England, and only eight out of twelve cities are occupied. The smashed windows are coloured. The family is too dark to afford the rent. "I said 'Good morning' to the ladies many years ago; she looked at me; she can't explain the feeling of removal. The children may be wrong; it may be against the law, but words frighten them." "Why the hell should they dare to have plaits in the hair?" The decent council flat is out of sight; the wife is too small; flattering one bedroom; the nasty neighbours could leave; the plaits are better in Paddington; the gentle Negro has one son crushed by smashed children. "But not at home – they're shy, after all – they've got to… I'm not going to… you say you wouldn't… we didn't realize Mrs Longville wouldn't mind next door, but then we wouldn't know, perhaps." She sat on the sofa, and the gentleman had his arm round her for ten years; she shouted she was born there; the camera smashed the photographer's mind; the scared children won the war with gentle manners; why should I speak when it's bad for them? The practice was to make the flat like everyone else. When they were given a nice flat with no distinction of tears everyone could see how this all started.

A NEARBY SLUM IS NOT PITIED; clothes over the floor; six prams allowed: loving in the neighbour's garden is better than playing in bed. The lawns for a time needed talking to: the children do this in quiet voice: "I am now hanging in space. Automatic me sallies downstairs and swerves around the nasty quiet. I am convinced of many monsters. In my face comes the funny face. I make big friends when I know my parents."

THE REST OF THE MORNING IS VERY HARD. Arching the back with particular skill, the boxing instructor tends to hit very hard as often as possible. "Then he started beating me on Saturdays. When I was six or seven he beat me – he would get so angry. I would stand against the garden fence and he would beat me, slashing as hard as he could. Oh yes, he got it off his chest that way, aware of the rest of my life."

THE GARDEN WENT ROUND FOR TEN DAYS. Tiny babies refuse to eat when beaten, ignoring the breast for the same reason. Only the mother dares not sleep, for fear of the salacious cry in the night. The floor rears itself up in strain and dies with the brown-paper parcel tied to the boards. Even those impersonal children crawl downstairs to wonder how long the rabbit will be there in the blue box, with its own nose twitching.

THE SECURITY OF A DIRTY ZOO. Find your stinking child sitting on food, building a nest of experience, committing suicide at the end of a chain.

THE CHILDREN HAVE BEEN EXHAUSTIVELY INVESTIGATED. A committee plans unpleasant experiments. They push them to the limit, each individual limit, using himself again and again. The ethics remain tricky. Their motivation is explained; some are over-keen to take part. After ten weeks of isolation, put the question: What makes them do it? This may mean they enjoy some technique of hidden disease. They are connected to a machine which works in a fairly unspectacular way. The actual sensation is of woolly slippers over the face. The clip on the nose sounds alarming; the effectiveness of instruments is fifty-fifty. Human subjects pay a shilling a ride. Ministry officials are not appointed; the medical idiot is enough.

THE EXCITEMENT OF LIFE. The longed-for box of chocolates. Very slowly eight boys and girls go to sleep together.

"WE HAVE A ROOF THAT BOTHERS. We have few things. We hope to live cheaper. How?"

NEW PAINT FOR SIX YEARS HAS NOT BEEN SEEN. "Without compensation we would not be here." The wallpaper is forbidden to telephone apologetically. The room is prepared to receive the mother, to prevent deterioration as far as possible. The control of the child is not worth the dirty stuff the mother left there. The first morning is unthinkable. The lively evening is shut on return; the nightmare was absolutely necessary; the electric plug is cut from below; the plastic hand has disappeared. Again the shaky morning comes unsuspecting; the rapidly opening window looks like the dawn – the exterior-looking wintry dawn that waits downstairs.

THE THREE PERIODS OF GLOOM; the time of the birds flying in V; the fleet swimming in the field of air in the column of rising air. It never stops officially. Drinking is the last resort, though the rainwater is occasionally dangerous. The people wept soup, drinking the world's heart. They love children; is it not strange they ran out of money?

THE BLOCK OF HOUSES WAS AN OVEN. Like a hospital, separated by fences, there was no sign of a room wrapped in thick sleep. The heat of flesh heard four strokes through the floor; the room was filled by a wall; the nine years felt heavy on the shoulder; the red basin of glass was covered by coal. Her hands noticed the tight gown tattooed by white soap, grey gums weeping with soap in them; the body moved the foot which slipped in childhood; the eyes watched the basin through the air. The window could see the man opposite; he was shouting information with his bones; the room breathed with slowness buttoning his jacket through the door; the feet in the room began yelling; the flat face was frightened by his arms in the middle of his clothes; the ceiling went on talking slowly fit to choke. He brought her down to the floor; yesterday the head moved in the cupboard. The coffee was boiled cabbage gradually; the words drowned in the bed whenever she liked, louder than anyone else in the warm bed. The expressionless moment: the soup colour downstairs under the wooden feet fallen in the room asleep in the iron oven to cover the fire at night. It was green with cleanliness; the sand and chairs on the wall were soldiers in the light room; the pink box filled the ceiling; the door was another leading to onions and hot coal pondering in the cupboard. The door appeared in the squat house, banging into the night asleep in the pit; the door opened onto yesterday's ground, swallowed in the corner, blown out and locked up, shutting the door behind; a last door banged in bed; the shadows folded their arms along the road.

and hundreds of numbers of trams on the road; and you have these poor guys swinging and beautiful; and he eats nuts like a dream; and straw is turned over the whole country – there isn't one house unexploited; everything loose would fall on the doorstep; he says "I've told you the dream – fall down, mock it"; he hates what it was – the arrogance of war in which he was obliged to show pity – when he lived in a loft for three blank years. Now he faces the freedom of the mother who would be an artist one day, each beginning with days locked up in freedom. When he came in he said "That is why I will go and eat bean soup" – back from the war, passionately painting his mother on the bed, asking where he had been.

THE DAY IS MARVELLOUS IN INDUSTRIAL LONDON. Every city is there in the land of Paddington, grey as plastic tomato.

The acres of pleasure cost fifty shillings a week, excluding food, electricity and nervous breakdown.

OTHER PEOPLE LIE DOWN, BUT THIS WIFE HAD HER SHOCK STANDING. She is too young for Britain. The bodies of newcomers are bought and sold, bit by bit, for green cheese and powdered milk. The wife wanted the whole house sprayed white; she was spending her time sleeping with a dog and three bloody cats; she was looking for a bit of land to raise vegetables. She said she had seen an advertisement for soil: "Now they've sent me the wrong sort of soil!" She offered her belly to the city three times a night, at four o'clock, six and eight.

THE MAN IN THE CAR HAD A QUICK SMILE WITHOUT A SMILE. She found the squeezed and concentrated movement exciting.

WHY NOT DRIVE OFF STRAIGHT AWAY? One and a quarter hours. How long between him picking you up? And you? He talked about people he knew. Are you married? Yes. Something. I've got something that would. Quieten you. Struggle. I shout for help. He terrify me. Face frightened me. I moved across. We talked for a bit. His manner changed. Physically I could have stopped him. Talking for a bit. After. Kept saying I wanted coffee. Didn't want coffee particularly. He let the driver's seat go. I fell back onto the passenger's seat. He just sat there for a while. The second time was he gentle? I didn't really. Notice? I was trying to push him off. Offered me a cigarette. I kept telling him he ought to go.

SHE DIDN'T. Discourage me. Went further. To see how she reacted. It wasn't a definite "no-go-away". Would have taken her. Minutes if willing. Yes. You know what I want. Wait to see. Kiss and cuddle.

IT WAS A COMPLICATED PLACE FROM ALL OVER THE WORLD, five colours on holiday, humming from a lorry. Now look back: the cars moved easily, as a man with big animals, restless, mobile. The careful glare is shaped aerodynamically, reducing the cost of exploitation. The apostles of speed despoil the atmosphere; the city is floating in foul gas, but "the entire town is suffused with natural charm". Two hundred grey people live on radiant platforms; the overwhelming success of pre-cast concrete cells recalls the splendour of a century ago.

THE MOTORCYCLE ATE A SEVEN-YEAR-OLD GIRL; a few people used a telephone.

A CERTAIN CAVITY LIKE A TOMB; the skin is left like a girl asleep. His hands climb up her, play a game with the shape of an idea faltering in the curve as he talks.

THEY HAD THE TEACHER DISMISSED. They frightened him by the lasting method – drawing the blood of the child.

THE BEAUTIFUL YOUNG LIVED IN EALING; the dog had a glamorous waistcoat; the princess cried in the fog; the child was asleep in her bed; she looked from the window, but it was not wide enough; the unthinkable window swam with nails; shouting children hung out flags which said things silently; the child changed little; she seemed very beautiful in the place, everywhere with portraits and flowers and gowns that gasped in velvet frames carefully tended in the old-fashioned way. So much greenery was deplorable. The shopping was no longer amusing. The Lord remained the same – a friendly chimpanzee. People came to dinner with a thousand advantages, when the bus passed the door before the war.

NOW THE SAD CITY CANNOT BEAR THE YOUNG GROUP THERE. It makes me think I'm forty, but I'm not sure. I know I'm going to end; I know I was born; I remember my youth in flat language. This is the first time I have studied architecture to still the tension. A vague gesture of empire crushes my stomach. I go to these parties for the genitals, the heart…

SHE HAD HER OWN WAYS, SHE TOLD ME. "My chief job was to look pleased." I have found five dazzling model-girls by the amateur method. I collect names to put in your eyes. The girls' idea of looks is to succeed in New York; they are new – very new. Sally in pictures likes to work well; people like English skin; fashion is still a trick; you have to highlight London; the idea is to wear paint at a party. You can't catch Marianne Faithfull – her mood is important. The end result is complete personality with the virtue of mouth. The melon-shaped personality of a first-class technician warms the director's heart: professional women look more female; the angelic mouth is an invisible export.

BOTTLES BULGED UNDER TARTAN SCARVES, and gin was consumed in the white-tiled lavatory. Certainly the Scottish scholars acted the part of conquerors, but the orgy of overcoats in the female premises looked like planned festivities. Their accomplishment was to colonize by force. With buttresses of alcohol after cheerless weeks of sober work, they tended to wish their revered parents in Northern Alberta.

A WARNING VOICE WAS RAISED ON BOTH SIDES OF THE ATLANTIC; the hazards of war lasted 35 years; the young people were not worried.

THEY LEFT THE TOWN AND TOOK A BUS TO EDINBURGH; they queued for dates on New Year's Eve, with the black flies grinning.

LIKE THE MAN IN TOLSTOY'S STORY, they were satisfied with a monthly ration of pretty girls each as large as the Ukraine. What the young man wants is most of the world; he finds it easy to be strong, provided he can seduce his great-grandmother.

THE MONOTONY OF RIVERS, immense things in Edinburgh, champagne in the back garden, 20,000 spermatozoa and this is all right. At half-past eleven the adored one in bed – all sleeping in one bed – they did not care for their companions – the foot odour became apparent.

THE PECULIAR PROVINCIAL CITY was shocked by spinach in a hotel room; the undergraduates were masters of the old world; T.S. Eliot was assumed to be a Martian; their future was to prevent the blowing-up of the galaxy; through the summer night they stuffed newspapers into bottles and knelt in private prayer.

MARIANNE FAITHFULL STARING AT 7.15 A.M., DOTTED WITH DEAD LEAVES, GREETING EVERYONE AT THE DOOR, brushing and burning the town – "We're so happy as it happens" – enjoying all morning with the boys. The phantom officer last year did not come. One knows what is going on: in the late afternoon teenagers drinking at parties again, maybe your best friend shuffles out of the kitchen, and here we go against the wall, praying to Oedipus with his two daughters. There is so much hash at the welfare agencies, the stuff is handed round – people arrive with wheelbarrows; cultured families prefer meditation as a substitute; the vast area of science maintains the leisure problem; people dump their garbage in the language laboratory. The seventeen-year-old is shallow, filled up every three months, keeping alive with sweet delight; freedom shows on her records; at the first passionate parties down there a crowd of young people hung on a tree one night with bored bottles of beer.

MEN WITH WOODEN CLUBS CONTRADICT ONE ANOTHER. Within a few days they return to London to learn how to kill properly.

THE TRAIN HOME TO CHARING CROSS SMELLED OF URINAL; this national problem instantly became a way of life: "Well – wasn't it nice?" No. They approached the corridors of houses. The waiting for cream and sponge cake was over.

THE CAPITAL INCREASES. From the train comes the sound of the hills; it is a red rhythm living there. The wealth of London does not wait. The hotel was not the same sixteen years ago.

TOP-LEVEL WINDOWS LIT WIDE GALLERIES; THE CHAOS WAS WIDENING; the palace was designed to close; everyone could see the end, everyone kept moving – we knew our chaos. About the city, over and against the city, the father seen as cloud shadow, the urban myth centred on the figure, the European recognized and overwhelmed, the great northern city communicates shock. You realize the wave moves on, atoms disappearing; the child killed – hung in the centre of the city square. Anyway, the children knew; there were so many of them; they could play their games without time limit or restriction.

EIGHT MONTHS AGO THE NEW DEEP CARPET WAS SCRAPED AND PAINTED. The dead-city miracle was better than ever. They had already forgotten what had happened. The city dignitaries had promised the central heating once again; the Government had given £300 for a library. Tanks had delivered guests to houses all over the town, with gifts for each shopkeeper and businessman. The fried housewife hunts the market regardless of season; asparagus breaks down kitchen walls, cooking rare fruits in fluorescent light. The scars on the slums were deep and formless. The big premises were fully functioning. The banks were still earning, and sometimes money at thirty-three per cent was rushing away with itself. For ten years people in truckloads had been taken off to sawdust-covered destruction; now they were split down the middle and loved by officers in smart uniforms. Dogs were dried and varnished; cats were saved; the centuries' muck this summer was cleared away. Books were collected in basements black with oil, the pages buckling slowly. A thousand dangerous pages were thrown on the fire. Grandiose schemes laid floors into the future; the sun burnt blue; for those who worked in small rooms the money was slow to come. Antique tables had more glamour than contemporary art; the museums alone had hope. The tragedy stretched over the family; all jewellery in the city belonged to the Church. For the first time the crucifix in the hospital was daubed with oil; the people had slept in mud for six hundred years. Thousands of walls were bulldozed for the people. There were only two cups in the new laboratory. The hotel was beautiful and welcoming for £50. Soldiers patrolled the ruins; they pinned medals on firecrackers. A thousand men gathered plastic strips to exchange for girls for sale in shops, tied together and placed upright, each face covered over. For the special display of money in the Gardens, fourteen million pounds arrived; there was so much goodwill – the names published and inscribed on a stamp. You can talk to the people; no one can accuse you of superficiality; the ministers sit in the ministries; the yellow restaurant squats on holiday waters; the culturally minded buy books; she wakes screaming in the morning; they may break down the door of her house; the city is glutted with money; the sky looks normal; it explains the growing feeling of fear.

THE PROMINENT BUILDING WAS CLAD IN ALUMINIUM SUN-VANES, which were polished at least once a day. The curious structure had wide shady roofs; each one collapsed while it was being built. Other perspectives were rising inside the fabric itself, which stood on slightly rising ground, and towering behind the main construction most of the block looked like something grandiloquent made of money. The slab-sided bone block contained no apartment smaller than a prestige project; the brilliant achievement contained the sky.

THE SIZE AND STYLE OF A DWARF WHO SPRANG AND PINCHED THE STRANGER, the millionaire impressed the spacious suite. On the edge of fresh roses every builder was going bankrupt. The dream of size was predictably inadequate for the nonsense dream-palace designed to show where the roses came from. The luxuriant imagination dazzled Paris – only the raised and covered roads convinced the excited buildings that they were wrong.

FOUR OR FIVE TIMES A DAY THE RECORDED VOICE IS VISIBLE FROM THE TALLER BUILDINGS. "Oh, don't go there" – twice a day across the road, from police officers investigating infiltrators. The local automatic experimental officers check their instruments sooner or later, each with a telephone and delicate equipment around the neck. They sit close to the measured mast, their life in the limelight, examining a small mechanism. One man inscribes numbers on a ticket of orange steel. On a fine day the men sit on the roof, full of blue, until the spots of rain fall on the toy windmill. The highest roof has three tin cans tied to it; the copper rain inside the cans relays messages by radio. John bursts his parachute and brings it down patiently to his office on the forty-fourth floor. Fourteen times a day he looks at the clouds and can tell you the time by counting the specs of rain in his eyes. Suspended from a tall government tower, a balloon soars to the other side of the world. (It travels to China and meets problems when it gets there.)

IN WASHINGTON THE NUMBERS OF PIGEONS SAILING ON THE WIND ARE USED FOR INFORMATION, as they whizz round the top of the Capitol. In a way it's scientific. The investigators can calculate the number of lawyers framing alibis, and decide whether to prepare a new dossier before lunch (their salad and sausage stands ready behind glass). A computer takes over from the men; personal news is the rare exception of the occasional day – there are devices by which they control it. The computer decides the pressure of the world; it produced future changes; man had ten ways to feed him; the radiosonde was faster than any existing; the mysterious balloon imitated reality for forty-eight hours. They study the charts in detail; next door rare instruments are used. None of them knows the sound of the language used by the rest of the world.

TREMENDOUS MONEY IS TRUE LIKE PRESIDENT KENNEDY, magnificent individual, altar joy working at winning belonging. Magically intimate feelings leap forwards into happy mouths. Five hundred sporting skills communicate directly. High-quality psychology operates on subconscious blocks. Natural people are developed by Arthur Sloan. The hidden eye in the office raises its hand when it wants a drink. The taste of western business says yes to the innocent. A million Americans in America alone; enthusiasm for America is planned; American joy – vitamin-enriched, protein-based, true.

THE CHAIRMAN OF THE AIR FORCE ABOUNDS WITH BOYISH ENTHUSIASM: he makes a special appeal for the young to be transported into the sky. "We need people able to spell, reliable witnesses of the sound of the ripped-off wings." Thirteen in one night volunteer for the adventure. Roger, who is eighteen, looks into the sky for six hours a day; he reaches for a drink at noon. The Chairman apologizes for being late; he thinks his pilots are missionaries; he quotes the names of the Gospels with particular emotion, with no interest in lesser people.

A BOTTLE OF WHISKY IS LOGICAL. The terrified senator tries to alleviate the disillusioned poor. His wife carried a bomb, her hair tied to the handle. Books and papers stop suffering. I think it's shameful to castrate the state attorney.

YOU EAT THE FORMULA. It makes you slim, more or less – normally. It has an excellent effect on what you don't eat. The idea is to consume your calorie intake. Food which swells is known to be good for you: biscuits, for instance, and steak. The taste of bread will give a lot of people a comfortable stomach. In 1965 he had two children cooked and tasted as an experiment; they tasted something like egg. Poached baby is a nice little meal – he is very secretive about the curious cooking process.

FOUR HUNDRED MILES BY MISSILE: FRANCE MUST HAVE HER OWN.

THE PARIS POP SINGER WAS HELD IN PRISON FOR TWO MONTHS; he broke with the Cominform;* his anti-totalitarian father changed his name and found work with the tourist trade. I wish Cardinal Stalin would die. God resigned from the party; he must have been an atheist at heart. The arithmetic director for three years was a communist, for five years the wrong kind of communist, who could not control himself, then for four more he was what the party wants, and then for thirteen he contradicted. The party wants how many more years?

DR ZHIVAGO WAS MURDERED ON THE WAY – the corpse was a foreigner; the governor replied: "I don't know." The

Doctor's family was abolished, the author lost; meanwhile, his father was walking home from prison.

PRISON IDEOLOGY WAS CLOSE TO HERESY, so he went to extremes of discipline; he was correct; he became an alternative candidate; his boots and papers belonged to the socialist alliance; the party remained in control of the right; the bureaucratic policeman arrested the whizz-kid politician; Noel Coward said "I'm not sure", with a portrait of Marx in his pocket (he had had a better life before the revolution); he had known Germans who were really good – now they could not be found; there were worse things planned for the future; he would become depressed in prison with other anarcho-liberal elements.

THE FRENCH AUTHOR LAID HIS GREY FACE ON THE MARBLE STAIRCASE OF THE PRIME MINISTER'S SALON; the successful poet had atomic power, smile of esteem; he had been a communist in Spain; he was asked to explain, politics on vague faces, tributes paid to his face – several thousand dollars – he is being paid by *Life*.

GOERING LAUGHED. He overkilled a second time and became angry. The arithmetic country has no leader. The best-selling radiation meter confuses inner thinking on important issues.

THE OPERATIONS ANALYST TRIPLE-CHECKED THE ACCURACY OF THE AIR FORCE ACCOUNTANT; the New York Government got on the hotline to Iceland; Russian space material was responsible for the attack on Rhode Island; the President wiped out North Carolina; the area office rejected the suggestion; action delayed from 9 a.m. till 11.30 p.m., then prolonged indefinitely; ten colleagues lost face, lectured on the destruction of peace; they would provide a clean war in place of dirty peace. The lesson of the bomb was to kill the President; press all his buttons, even if this meant his hands were raised and his reputation lowered. The importance of planning five years ago against Chinese policy: publicity changed the approach to hydrogen bombs – a softer sell to improve the image. Alarmed by graphs, he refuted thinking; he believed discussion created personality differences which would not arise on an uninhabited planet.

IN HIS CELLAR THE RICH ALCOHOLIC ATTEMPTED TO REBUILD SOCIETY. His consultants corresponded with Government officials in each case, and concluded that the H-bomb would not be a catastrophe for the chiefs of staff. A system of H-bombs attached to boot straps would restore a nation's dynamism; a rigidly programmed computer might emerge as a great power; Russia would lose her credibility; German humans would be used as slaves; Kennedy would withdraw from the United States; the world would decline into crazy history.

A DOT ON A GRAPH IS HAPPENING.

POLICE SHOUT OUT A STRING OF WORDS as they march down corridors. No one spoke as they dragged the body from the rim of the great stadium. The chief of police was prepared for next winter; his men lined up for duty. All this was being rehearsed; he had disciplined some of them; their equipment was ready to go; his assistant gave out tickets for the show; everyone bought one; the veterans demanded two.

ENDLESS EXCLAMATION MARKS FORM A TOWER FOUR YEARS HIGH, REACHING TOWARDS THE GREY.

THE POLICE HIT THE STUDENTS FIRMLY AND BROKE THEM UP; the swear words made these guys mad; they curse together, policemen yelling; short-skirted girls get hit where it really hurts; you can bang them against the wall when we beat them later, cracking bones every few seconds, a ton of muscle driving into peach and honey; he shoved his hand in, hammering athletic; they cry as they hit their necks.

THE OCEAN GASHED THE LONG WHITE GLASS; the sailors rolled right over; the pane of glass was blind; three nurses on bicycles ate pie and ice cream with a twist of the hips down the lavatory; long pink baby under the arm, the physical husband asleep on a heap of parcels. The vegetarian girl with yellow hair winked at the Baptist minister in the bright shirt; she didn't understand the conventions – she had seen his cock from 300 miles away, playing with figs, eating ribs of beef with her nail clippers, plaiting her hair in the lavatory; she fed her baby the end of his wet cigar; the cow rolled over; with twelve big pieces of coconut bar, sick on the grass, she posed on a heap of parcels; photograph her pussy for ten dollars; her lips moving with the landscape, leaving off her winter silver buttons, she met two fellas suffering from haemorrhages, and suchlike crippled hippies.

SCORCHED EYES FULL OF WHIRLWINDS; the old dark difference teases you; lorries talk of work; caged assassin in an uneasy place; drunks for sale; a starched-blue gun in a pitch-black window; grabbing documents and pecan delights. The assassin could buy a Mustang and skid along the western rim; a man's got his hands on the back wheels; the uniform escape route; you need to know the highway's questionnaires, pattering on about curing racial unrest. Who was the driver behind the soft American car? She seemed to be giving him some relief; the piece of pie alive with pickle; guns everywhere, kneeling with relief, Mustangs everywhere, cops pining to grow up, evidence of yearning, the driver driving westwards into the land itself, seven, eight, yellow and blue highway; I'd shoot locomotives, a black new Mustang, rocks in mad shapes; this guy gave me trouble; it keeps the costs up; he stops to eat a wax cigar; he paid extra for the waitress; the explosive mark on her thigh: "I know I'll end up dead."

LEAN DEATH IS A CONFLICT BETWEEN MONKEYS; the word has seventeen letters. Monkeyshock of deliberate approach; a wife fifty years in the house; grass inside the kitchen, trees at the birth of the baby. The parents' coats are taken away because things have gone wrong in the connecting corridor; birth is expected at any time now – birth is a triumph of climbing and roaming, spontaneous escape. I have entered birth and survival, equipped with ropes; at the social level climbing is the principle of difficult living.

INTERVIEWED IN CAGES, madmen tell the world: fists flail to hammer the wall, the head is built in hate. BLAST those men who have the name of parents; DISGUST tears them apart, SPECTACULAR MONSTERS,
TWENTY-THREE THOUSAND DISCIPLINED ROWS of animals fifty miles north. FLUMP FLUMP FLUMP FLUMPFFF.   KON. KNOCK THEM DOWN.

ON THE HOT BRIGHT DAY OF ATOMIC CONSTERNATION, they furled the night. The meteor snapped the end of the centuries, the clouds shouted and pulled their shaped nets in haste, tearing the sky before dawn. The puppets in the city of low wood and paper grabbed paper madly and covered their eyes; Christianity went on as always towards their shore. The old men, birds' heads wild with fear of political menace, were wary of the sudden intruders, but on the beach the women appreciated the dramatic foreigners; they went with buckets of water to the American arrival on the self-conscious doorstep to buy the country. In the shops the bright day came quietly; the comfortable officials were well beyond reach; the crucifixions were done indoors; the slaughter stared at the black and gold for forty days, while ornamented women attempted to live by trade. Their silk night series of silks shivered with fires lit on the head; everyone returned from abroad towards the ocean of impotent seclusion; old women along the coasts blew the intruders away, and these strange sights said no.

ONLY THE AMERICAN ANTHROPOLOGIST SURVIVED. He was busy on a good thing.

LITTLE IS KNOWN. Man hides. Ape qualities grow. Avoid the female. Change. Low, thin, with a jaw and teeth. Dog head. He eats eggs. Hunt animal. Pain. Shriek.

HAMSTERS ARE MIGHTY PUPILS. Instead of memory they spend years of life in a box.

GRASS SKY. Green sun. White distant sound.

CRYSTALLIZED BLACK DELIRIUM, metal-white terror, singular stone mania, mineral illness, inexplicable earth, hills of stone, changed leper, green sun, dense bright-green swollen bodies, pulverized heart, heart thump, illness, science at each step, give oxygen, horizon on the margin of a strange thing, the use of the knife.

ATOMIC RETURN TO THE ENORMOUS THICKNESS OF ICE A MILLION YEARS BEFORE THE SOLID ICE DRIFTED APART. The theory of distances and patterns of drift. Quartz ice, sack cloud, storm force. The answer is impossible.

THE BRIDGE OF EARTH, the movement of the roughly triangular land, link between lands. The high face will turn; the road will have been a slim column of extreme lightness into the hillside; it will turn quickly over the sloping land, concave lower down in spite of the concentration of concrete. The pattern of tight curves can be anticipated; the grey-green lane will resemble the natural flow.

THE WOODEN CITY NO LONGER EXISTS as the green children approach. The child has changed. Weakness ensures continuing shock; patches of bright money float in mattresses; the children sell guides to the old city. "We could earn more at games." Life becomes meaningless deliberately – get a job repeating rhythmically, paint the mind clean.

POVERTY ENDS IN VIOLENCE. They make a revolution for entertainment. The big-money kids catch the goddam boy; now they go murderous, meet death the day before.

WATCH THE BREATH OF PATIENTS. The hospital has a temperature of 120 degrees; the blood flow slackens. The hospital was struck by lightning. The five-ton lorry stuffed bread into her dress. The large families made their big move.

VISIBLE EMOTION GOES SLOWLY BROWN; bundles slide continuously in efforts to avoid the years. The situation is expensive: urgent applications for washing machines are accumulating. Reporters split families with well-constructed questions; the doctors would like to see more response; the threads again are running in the air; the baby yells up the steep ramp hour after hour. The two sides cross; a counter-movement cautions; the trickle disturbs the even flow; tens of soldiers guard the area.

MRS CARTWRIGHT WAS TRAMPING THE PAVEMENT WITH OVER £2,000 after an order by the Leek County Court that cash and cheques could not be used without permission. Her post-office money was lost by Mr Harry Clarke, the husband of a wholesale greengrocery concern. "The public are obviously in favour," said His Honour, before he climbed into his telephone and drove off.

BUT SUCH IMPRESSIONS CAN BE MISLEADING. In America today there are more than a hundred churches open for the thirty-three million rich today. Religious books attract the well-educated; the best three million are published by the Church, and Christians are able to get higher certificate on Sunday. The certificates are obtained by force or fraud – the price of orthodoxy is high. The sharp and clever are sold in hell, and heaven looks shifty to some, but the Church is used to people who believe that thought has ceased.

THE PAINTER HAS EATEN THE JUNGLE; the dream of the rocking-chair dream has evolved; the theme of traffic into street; the tight pattern of poles around the people; imagine people rewoven a thousand times; he is now deep in his Victorian bed to sleep in the street instead of working; his dream-bed seems ugly in the road; he does not count his love; the remote new is shown in summer; the rare is rarely found in town; you should be in Europe by the roadside; there is an edifice – go there! In spite of himself in autumn, his bicycle glorifies the dream in mocking it; the ten dazzling towns he knows; the ten names too are stolen from the railway; he has been smeared with the extended parts of his dream. Of course he doesn't like the political idea, the electric one at the top. Pop soothes women with light; he excludes them from his dream; nobody need be sold in his world. The dollars museum is all around there is, there let the poor thunder; the dream paints new signs for two

years; he smiles when questioned; there is enough space for two
to lie together; inseparable from his dream the wealth flows
in friends together, the same numbers of gold and minerals,
friends in barns together crammed with wheat to burn; the
significance of human abundance photographed by *Vogue* with
the name of the motor oil quoted in conjunction with every
place. Look at the next scene:

THE MAN ON THE ROAD WAS ACROSS THE PLAIN; he could
make the ground black, and the sea-ice was a flat tree on the
straight land. His coat was held at home, and he was cold with
intense day for an hour. The red air was pain. The cut fence shut
the track; the grass had a roof on; the light was a smoke eye
caught by a block of light; the hanging sound penetrated the
pit, the fire a shadow emptying. The man was a horse waiting;
sleep worked the lever; the eye said who he was; the dark shook;
nothing interrupted the pit choked by coughing. The ground
was over there. The big horse with six legs was blown up by
fire, the squat head sticking up ready to devour the world. He
saw there was nothing on the road in the morning, no door.
The horse shouted misery in America; the howling darkness
named the people; the western burning threatened; the horse
was harnessed to empty tubs; the young space blew death by
the hundred and the oven burnt blue in the sky of iron. Time
had brought three sheets of metal and the glad accident had a
strangler's face. The name grinned three times when the skin
of the frog was roasted. The fit of white light with blue neck
and hands like a horse; stone ears scraped the pit, then a man's
legs perished and a doctor fell out of a bucket. The foot could
not move without shouting, and the hammer went on banging
the carcass slowly. He had known the strong flattened by rocks;
three sons had got out of his skin, and the kids found something
to eat. The windows felt cold as they were lowered into the
pit. There's money! The horse had started again downward,

the journey wiping the foam off the wind. The man moved in a ball in space roasted by fire; a dog in darkness, dead ovens red with history, its meal of flesh.

HARD TIMES FOR A CUP OF TEA! The wild Irish sing down the Edgware Road, while others are waiting by the mountains to be caught by soft voices in tired mist. The bays are filled with fishermen; the old life is brightly painted; a mile trip is a big event planned for Father: "Will ye no be comin' by train?"

CHRIST STAYED GOSSIPING FOR A FEW DAYS in the cluster of villages; the place had a cultural outline, the homes of zodiac signs. He journeyed six or seven miles: the rich travel only when things go well. He wrote his book about the world – the idea of the parallel world, the world of order in the future, preserved in a book. He was attached to the old world of interest in minds and lives, sometimes more, sometimes nations, classes and so on. The prejudice swerved towards its target; the blast turned on him with force. But he kept separate from the world of fixed interests. His old world replaced it.

BEST RELIGIOUS SYSTEM IN THE WORLD. AVRO State Service. Big staff, Catholic enterprise, against the excesses of socialists. All schools and doctors in one system. Christians have manifest faults, but their aggressive approach, their ruthlessness, transmits profits from far afield.

A PERSON IS HIS NAME. When he needed a new name, he turned however indirectly towards bread and wine. When he had been reinforced by his family name, the remote midway name, when asked his name, he had heard the slight danger sound of the high accordion. Now Jesus was taking chances. He needed the radio link with revelation. He remained for a period of eighteen months a distance of several thousand miles. Finally he needed neither name nor food. He had a glimpse of the only compost a man's house needs, and he in his turn was allowed a glance under the warm surface. The spirit came to call. He responded as to a woman, with the type of behaviour in which it is a dance, holding together with no rivalry. It was also secret. The maternal caress of watchful warmth. It ended in violence softly. The original family of man did not forgive the other. The blood improved in wood like wine; it cost nine shillings a bottle, was sent twenty miles away, given the identity of God.

there being of glass on walls, clouds over, glass cube but this is rare, composed of cubes, they fit flat, in the frame of brass, glass, coloured glass, in order that the light should shine through, yes this is so, each one of thousands, the effect of spacing, irregular, the effect is almost dull, the size changes, flesh in glass, in the form of wrinkles, parchment, with green or red written across, grouped, important, Church propaganda, confined to windows, use glass of particular richness, you can see below, allow this dome, the shape of church, allow curved space, the lines of an octagon, use fewer, the best, apple blue you see, please the people, attempt illusion, crucifixion of the frontal figure, the theme is refined, very graceful, please as well as strike, you have to look up, hinting below, began with the eye, globe of eye, separate the two, wider, humanity of head droops a little, so gracefully, remembered, theme repeated, bring the mind, within, procession of people, tribute to the king, propaganda, presenting gifts, bring God, for a moment, less in size, minute, moved about, the only way, in larger form you find fascinating, particularly in decline, it costs less, personal piety, new style, stone source, astonishing quarries, the experiment succeeded, obviously, suited by complexity, a colourful thing, it is sensational, the pattern within, the individual, worth examining, it has character, if you look, you will find Him, it is no accident, this is where you belong

now you ask
the thing would collapse
the archbishop is certain
a person killed in Turkey
he tells the tradition received
this takes you back
the meaning does not turn
dead memory
now how they came to the
nothing depends on what
after all
he never assumes
in some sense
the shattering thing
and then the thing stopped
standing and talking
this is continuous
say on the seashore
there seems to be
he was buried
he has got up
took his clothes with him

no reason
the essence of the matter
you must believe there was
how reliable is the evidence
when you come to think of it
the strength of the evidence
on physical remains
a new situation
conviction is a question
happened
yet he never mentions
we will disintegrate
what we should call
vaporized
finished
allowing them to touch
don't you think
this to a lot of people
elaborate stuff
he was dead
revived
they would have stripped
him

suggests to me strongly
at best one might say
but for me
the fact that matter and energy
it opens one's mind
becoming
all sorts of contradictions
in a strange way
has been found
generalizations
it goes beyond the particular

reconstituted
some kind of possibility
great shock
are equivalent
there are possibilities
not solid not permanent
this thing
experimental
laws of science
man-made
nonsense

you would say he is alive   because you see
we have to   the classical example
everybody knows about electrons without seeing one
because the effects were   a long time ago
yet   what does this mean
when he was asked   I think
to be subjective   as a person
and this is what I believe   firmly
in mental images   in pictures
and I think that hmm   an agony
and yet   fundamentally
but to him   I feel it so because the fact
one knows   in a sense it never
existed   what it comes down to is
his moral position   I find myself
like his or like I thought   his was
extraordinary experiences so near me
although I knew   like another person
like my husband next to me I had such a wonderful
and the joy   and all I could say was
and this was an experience it was so real
a symbolic statement   in the sense that
obviously
yes but there have been   instances
but presumably it seems to
  me   I should have thought it was
unlikely   what one person said
it depends on what you   do not think
so far as we know   when we die
people say that   very happy and content
people make statements   that indicate
I might interpret   inside us in some sense
or another   I don't mean literally
all one can say is   here is an instance

how do they explain
I would think that
of presences
it doesn't seem to me
as a body
no

they certainly
people have seen all kinds
all this kind of thing
I can't see the end
as a human being

WHEN THE TIME CAME FOR HIM TO GO to a place where he was needed he explained that this requirement limited the possibilities in that the circumstances would create their own environment ultimately qualifying the manner in which he would or would not execute the exceptional tasks burdens and functions appropriate to his intangible and contradictory situation. The ignominious conclusions resultant and consequent on instantaneous conversion created an equation of spontaneity which obscured the necessary impossibility of significant action.*

THE STRANGEST THING IN THE SKY JUST NOW IS THE STARS. Possibly visible as faint blue stars, they are precise in the sky.

AROUND THE EARTH THE PLANETS: each marked the state of the modern scratch-signs in the sand. After twenty-two days the Pope will descend from the why. He said that getting and fitting the crown would be a major task; his voice faltered; one of his girls appeared; he was very sorry, but he had had a good year; he did not want to be singled out; it was a team job; he was superbly backed by society (although he wore a Party badge, he was not and never had been a member).

The cone
electricity
simultaneity
intergalactic intelligibility (so many eyes)
research which leaves intact
the attack on lives

Bobby Baker
Baby Boko

GOOD BOYS DISCOVER NEW CONTINENTS. The blue steel nutshell starts calmly. Ten machines tell a good story. The dangerous trap is a slight misfortune. The craft runs away from earth. The volunteer for a few minutes pretends the pressure is greater. Astronomy makes him stagger slightly; he needs oxygen between the stars. The sun mystery has two eyes – green and blue; this bright thing because he is happy has the silent, beautiful body of a woman in a newspaper; he looks at her, defenceless. Beyond the air is something else too far away from Earth, where it becomes impossible to hide, his feet in ice for four years. The distant human watches his health intently, to detect the moon anxiously asking questions. Gods and heroes die in space; the explorer does not think of it. In 1988 in the sky in the morning – his eyes on a stick in space. He says yes for fear of failing. The attraction of the moon is 150 miles long; streams of moon provide the opportunity for seismic activity; the moon's heat is enormous; the moon's face is perfect boiling water; no, the moon is replica of rock.

THEY WANTED TO STRAP HIS LEGS AS AT BIRTH; minute jolts and gleams delivered into blue space like surprised eyes heavy with gold and dollars knocking around for years.

THE BRILLIANT SCIENTIST FROM THE SPACE AGENCY scrapes eggs from the skin.

MINUTE BY MINUTE, THE TECHNICAL FACES LOOK AT HIM.

LOOKED FOR HIS LEADERS. NO REPLY, NO REASON. Stars became mysterious chandeliers above dark members of an unfriendly family. After the burnt frenzy in the area that separated the narrow dark room from the back of the craft he had no doubt. The transformer was burnt out, and that statement was made from comprehension that his craft was a room without its own plant. That did matter. That was where the deficiency lay; the only part of the story that was not news. The young scientist excused the reporters who did no work; all had made the prophecy of failure; to ignore them was to fall from a tower into a trap. The absurd words meant simple death. A piece of steel was folded into the curved roof. In that, a minor error was made: it did not fit. The violent pattern of green disappointed and fatigued, and in the end the yellow-and-green edge caused disaster. The news was not a hoax; the flies buzzed in and out with sadness. The trip was definitely on, and would go on. The barbaric and religious photograph of the President became the true goal. The group died at the stroke of prestige absurd against a wall. The yellow colour of successful dust meant nothing.

HIS MOTHER SPOKE ITALIAN. She had five pieces of bread. The time was the end of the month. Pieces of evil outdoors; inhuman beings in stainless steel polished by the twelve-foot sun; the colour of the sun was dull green, the colour of common nature under the influence of science, and don't forget that nobody understands.

FIX THE POSITION OF THE RADIO ASTRONOMERS MORE PRECISELY.

MEN ARE OPENING THE MOON. Streams of wheels have springs of space. The rim of the system was the wide discovery of unintelligent activity. Lovely men remained untouched by many winds from space. His vehicles have enormous wheels. Individual effort evaporates in space. A million years of rain reflect the skill of space. His perfect skin will be water-cooled; his undergarments bear the marks of convulsive birth; advantage can be taken of his need to stay cool. Inside, the lesson is learnt without expression. There is no gloom. The white kitchen defines the cotton-contemplating man as cool as cotton. Like a plump young girl it is possible to make everything up. The cream silk conversation lies on the surface; the mind totally engages the calm tragedy; the mind turns pages; there are flowers at the limits of comprehension; gauge the outlines once again; again the complications have always been calm; it was even the family drabness in the plain landscape; the face of decay; fragmented intellect; the American failure is no surprise; in his mind the personal death is fifty years ago; his brother dead, he has no urgency, his habit is gone; five years past he had nowhere to go; now he is left, man as man.

THE PERFECT WREATHS GIVE INTENSE SATISFACTION. Stomachs take risks with highly intelligent champagne. Inspired by space, he received a medal for working for the sons of the rich. Like the gladiators he risked his blood, and throbbing spectators expect their sons to follow him.

AS LONG AS HE STAYS IN HIS CHAIR, happy in the clutches of the air, to risk his life twice. (You rarely find people on the moon.)

Characters

Waitress
Drunks
Chef
Priest
Italian waiter
American woman
Eamonn Andrews
Police
Ladies in gaiters
Children
Babies
Duke of Windsor
Vice-Admiral
Bolsheviks
Miss Hueth
Scottish sexologist
Housewives
Intellectuals
Criminals
Bishops
Archdeacon
Duke
Chief Constable
Widow
Queen
Household Cavalry
Barbra Streisand
Mrs Kennedy

Jesus
Billy Graham
Mary
Betty Lou
Mrs Davey
Persian girl
Romanian dean
British Council
Africans
Prime Minister
Terrorists
Reporters
Theodora
Models
Prostitutes
God
Negro
Jimmy Anderson
Detectives
Riot police
Groscinski
Marianette
Daddy
Immigrants
Mike Canaletto
Agitators
Cassius Clay
Russians

Painters
Dylan Thomas
Photographer
Princess
Designer
Osteopath
Colonel
Weirdies
Indian
George Harrison
Philosopher
Nurses
Salvation Army
Orphans
Rolling Stones
Matron
Barbara
Mrs Martwell (who saw the
   ghost)
Boys
Tough women
Guardsmen
Millionaires
Director-General
Soldiers
Magistrates
Accountants
Burglars
Frederick Forsyth
Diplomats
Baby-minders
Window cleaners
Archbishop
Spiritualist

Lolita
Bicyclist
Theatre-goers
Marlene
Bill
Kitty
Knight, Frank and Rutley
Council officials
Norwegians
Lord Cornwallis
Anarchists
Chinese
Texan general
Communists
Mother
Mickey Mouse
Minnie Mouse
Celts
General Westmoreland
Royal Horticultural Society
Chinese girls
Fusiliers
Captain
Buddhists
Fanatics
Stalin
Chief of police
Butcher
Sculptor
Plumber
Tramp
Bandits
Marxists
Property developer

Industrialist	Mussolini
Landlords	Commonwealth Cricket Club
Gangsters	Swiss Army
Governor	Policeman called Lilian
Salesman	Gunman
Voyeur	Telephone operator
Maureen	Scots Guards
Chauffeur	Peter Sellers
Park-keeper	David Frost
Homosexuals	Gypsy Rose Lee
Tennis players	Yvette Mimieux
Girl in the bath	Sam
Connoisseurs	Sergeant major
Dwarf	Gardeners
Censors	Annabel
Sex maniacs	Mother of twins
Right-wing MP	Torturer
Karl Kaspar	Transvestite
English girl	Pilots
Actress	Earl
Film Director	Kath
Heart specialist	Welfare worker
Kasparak	Mrs Longville
Professors	Boxing instructor
Prisoners	Ministry officials
Headmaster	Boozers
Farmer	Vicars
Dostoevsky	Bishop's daughter
James Joyce	Naked women
Patients	Mrs Murphy
Mortician	Petrol pump attendant
Lord Chief Justice	Countess
Bride	Ulysses
Pope	Mayor

Cameramen
Bankers
Byzantine spectators
Brigitte Bardot
Jack Kennedy
Marlon Brando
Cripples
Astronauts
Painter's mother
Marianne Faithfull
Students
T.S. Eliot
Oedipus
Arthur Sloan
Air Marshall
Dr Zhivago
Noel Coward
Goering
Malraux
President
Vegetarian
Sailors
Madmen
Mrs Cartwright
Others

Note on the Text

The text in the present edition is based on the first edition of *Babel* (Calder & Boyars Ltd, 1969). The 'Characters' section was written by the author and included in the original volume, so no efforts have been made to add to or subtract from the list for this new edition. The small capital letters beginning each section (or lack thereof) have also been replicated from the original edition, to preserve the understanding which can be derived from the point at which these "headlines" end and the text begins. The spelling and punctuation have been Anglicized, modernized and made consistent throughout.

Notes

p. 79, *the Duce*: "Leader" (Italian). A common name for Mussolini.

p. 125, *Cominform*: A common name for the Information Bureau of the Communist and Workers' Parties.

p. 138, *When the time... significant action*: The punctuation from the original edition has been retained in this block, since the constructions are clearly supposed to be redolent of legal language.

Dreamerika!, Alan Burns's fourth novel, first published in 1972, provides a satirical look at the Kennedy political dynasty.

Presented in a fragmented form that reflects society's disintegration, *Dreamerika!* fuses fact and dream, resulting in a surreal biography, an alternate history which lays bare the corruption and excesses of capitalism just as the heady idealism of the 1960s has begun to fade.